HAUNTED

With the same editor

Phantom Lovers
Stories of Haunted Inns
Ghosts in Country Villages
Ghosts in Country Houses
When Churchyards Yawn
Stories of the Strange and Supernatural
Stories of the Macabre
Stories of the Night
Stories of Horror and Suspense
Stories of the Occult
Haunted Cornwall
Cornish Ghosts

HAUNTED TRAVELLERS

Edited by
Denys Val Baker

WILLIAM KIMBER · LONDON

This anthology first published in 1985 by
WILLIAM KIMBER & CO. LIMITED
100 Jermyn Street, London SW1Y 6EE

ISBN 0 7183 0544 2

Photoset in North Wales by
Derek Doyle & Associates Mold, Clwyd
and printed in Great Britain by
Biddles Limited, Guildford, Surrey

Contents

		Page
	Introduction	7
I	Double Crossing *by Rosalind Wade*	9
II	Station Cab *by J.C. Trewin*	29
III	The Saracen's Stick *by Fred Urquhart*	38
IV	All in the Mind *Chris Simons*	55
V	The Labyrinth *by R. Chetwynd-Hayes*	61
VI	A Descent into the Maelström *By Edgar Allan Poe*	88
VII	The Day Trip *Patricia Daly*	105
VIII	Poor Kate *by Mary Williams*	115
IX	The Coastguard *by Lanyon Jones*	126
X	A Trip to the Forest *by Derek Stanford*	146
XI	The Lerryn-Brown Line *by Meg Buxton*	158
XII	Voice from the Past *by Denys Val Baker*	169
XIII	Lost Journey *by A.L. Barker*	176

Introduction

My previous anthology of ghost stories, *Phantom Lovers*, was a collection of tales of departed lovers who return to haunt their loved ones; thus the theme for this new collection seemed to follow on quite naturally for aren't journeys said to end in lovers' meetings? The travellers in these stories, however, are not quite so fortunate. Their encounters either during or at the end of their travels, whether they be by foot, train, coach or boat, are rather more sinister than a lover's kiss ...

For contributions to *Haunted Travellers* I would like to make the usual acknowledgements: to the authors for 'Double Crossing' by Rosalind Wade and 'Station Cab' by J.C. Trewin, both written for this collection; to the author for 'The Saracen's Stick', first published in *The Twilight Book* edited by James Hale, (Gollancz, 1981); to the author for 'All in the Mind' by Chris Simons written for this collection, to the author for 'The Labyrinth' by R. Chetwynd-Hayes first published in *The Elemental* (Fontana, 1974); to the author for 'The Day Trip' by Patricia Daly, written for this collection; to the author and William Kimber & Co for 'Poor Kate' by Mary Williams from *Where Phantoms Stir* (William Kimber, 1976), to William Kimber & Co for 'The Coastguard' by Lanyon Jones from *The Seven Deadly Sins* (William Kimber, 1977); to the author of 'A Trip to the Forest' by Derek Stanford, written for this collection; to William Kimber & Co for 'The Lerryn-Brown Line' by Meg Buxton from *No Earthly Reason* (William Kimber, 1980); and for 'Voice from the Past' by Denys Val Baker, published in *The Secret Place* (William Kimber, 1977); and to the author for 'Lost Journey' by A.L. Barker written for this collection.

I

Double Crossing

Rosalind Wade

How many people have the experience of a recurring dream? If the theory is correct that dreaming is the manifestation of a subconscious thought process, it would seem that the dream must have its origins in something that has actually occurred. This kind of retrieval from the limbo of the half forgotten could be acceptable while the brain slows down in slumber; but what if there is no identification with the immediate or distant past? In my case, it was the image of a house which repeated itself in dreams throughout my life; a rather distinctive style of architecture on four storeys, with narrow dormer windows and a flight of steep stone steps leading to the front door. It seemed to overlook a lake or river, for the sound of splashing water was always an accompaniment of the dream, and on either side of the house were giant, crouching creatures of no recognisable species.

That apart, the type of house could have been found in a variety of places; a chalet on the Swiss mountain side, a century-old flour mill in Hampshire, the Keats-Shelley Memorial house in Rome or one of the brick-built workshops in Tyne-and-Wear. As in my life travel played an important part I looked around constantly for the house. I never found it, and in the end I gave up trying. So, when I set out one April evening to journey from the Republic of Ireland to Wales, the dream was not in my thoughts at all. The trip did not begin particularly well. A local train had run into trouble with an engine breakdown at Bally Hinton. There were a number of

Irish soldiers waiting on the platform, going, it was said, to Israel to join the International Peace Keeping Force. They were young, untried and looked sheepish in response to the send-off organised for them. This took the form of raucous singing by a local pop group, accompanied by a banjo. But presently the officer in charge shepherded his men onto the train which was now ready to leave.

There was one first-class coach. I appeared to be the sole passenger prepared to indulge in this luxury. I had settled down to savour my solitude when I realised that after all I was not going to be alone. A woman was sitting immediately opposite to me, a strange-looking person, dressed all in black, offset by a straw hat decorated with limp feathers and a velvet scarf. Her hands, gnarled either by rheumatism or hard toil, lay motionless in her lap. Although not by any means a large woman, she had a dominating presence and I felt considerable annoyance that she had chosen to sit so close to me when there were other vacant seats. I wondered whether I would move? Tentatively, I gathered up my possessions. It needed courage and I began to think of excuses, for obviously, she had anticipated my base intention.

'Don't go,' she commanded me briskly. 'You are quite all right where you are.'

She spoke with a gutteral, foreign accent. I was surprised by her general air of autocracy. 'We're getting away, at last,' she went on, 'Sit back. Keep quiet and the time will pass quickly enough.'

She produced some crochet work from a bag and began to deploy the hook expertly. I watched fascinated as little rosettes appeared as if by magic. And then, as an alternative to staring at her, I turned to look out of the window. It was a sodden landscape saturated with recent rains. The inclement weather hastened the onset of night.

'It will be quite dark soon!' the woman observed rather sententiously. Her voice seemed to reverberate, as though through a long tunnel.

I made no response to this superfluous comment. It was still possible to make out a few landmarks; a small, squat church, half shrouded by the still bare branches of an enveloping elm, a three-humped bridge and the looming excrescence of a plateau-topped hill. Lights flickered in cottage windows and I wondered how people endured such isolated lives? Now, the train gathered speed. The voices of the young soldiers became muted while my companion continued her monologue remorselessly. I could neither hear nor understand a half of what she was saying and found my attention focussed upon her mouth. She seemed to have a loose front tooth, which had made a niche for itself on her lower lip. It reminded me of a woman who had once, for a brief spell, been my governess, so long ago that I had not thought consciously about her for many years. Her name was Mademoiselle Haute, and my recollections of her, such as they were, were far from pleasant. I recalled my dismay when this person was introduced to me in the drawing room of our house at Queenstown, or Kobv as it is now called. Sensing my reluctance she went into the defensive and almost dragged me upstairs to the nursery for tea. I screamed to my parents to rescue me but they merely urged me not to be discourteous to a stranger, and there the image faded, for I could not remember what happened when we sat down to our first meal together. So long ago, so unimportant at this moment in time, and yet my throat felt dry with fear at what must have been my first experience of insecurity.

We were almost at the end of the first part of the journey. I gathered up my possessions as we approached the station. People began dismounting from the train and the army personnel were marched off swiftly in the direction of the quay. An unpleasant shock awaited us. We had run into a heavy rain-storm and the platform was a shallow sheet of water. No porters were available. It seemed an endless trek towards the gangway. The boat rocked gently on her moorings, with a promise of greater disturbance to come. I found that I was shivering at the prospect of the storm-bound channel crossing and tried to master my obsessive fear of drowning, with the grey-green waters closing over my head. Briefly, I glimpsed my companion as she caught up with me.

'You should wear your bag over your shoulder,' she admonished, 'It takes the strain.'

I ignored the comment and hastened away from her up the

uncomfortably perpendicular gangway.

Although the journey was a brief one, I had reserved a first-class cabin which, though a double, had been let to me as a single for an increased fee. I wondered whether it had been wise? The cabin was situated on a very low deck and was intensely claustrophobic, despite some primitive ventilation. I examined the life-jacket. It would not be worthwhile to undress. Muffled sirens sounded. We were about to pull out from the quay, if indeed we had not already done so. I lay down, trying to let my body move with the swing, concentrating on the pleasant things in my life. Perhaps I came blessedly near to dozing? But not for very long. In the dim light of a naked electric bulb I saw that the cabin door was opening to admit – horrors of horrors – the woman on the train. She entered purposefully, dumped her bag on the floor and began to undress. I must have made some protest for she answered me sharply:

'Go to sleep. No need to stare at me. I'm the same with or without my clothes on.'

Maybe she thought she had mastered me? If so, she was mistaken. I sat up on the bunk and ordered her out of the cabin. She took no notice and began to wash her face and neck in the *cabinet de toilette*, making weird spluttering sounds rather like an ostler sluicing down a favourite horse. The effect of her raddled skin and pouting breasts was quite revolting. I got up off the lower bunk; half afraid that she would bar my way, but her body did not seem to offer any impediment and then, mercifully, I was out in the corridor, a horrible cavern of a place with vague distant clanging sounds and an odour of metal and vomit. There was only one attendant on duty, a weary looking individual by no means eager to listen to my complaints.

'If you have paid for two bunks the cabin is yours, to be sure. No one has any right in that cabin but you yourself.'

'But there *is* someone,' I shouted, above the mounting wind.

'Then you should tell her politely to go away. It is a female, I presume?'

Would he come and tell her, for me? No, his duties were too pressing because, and he lowered his voice to a whisper, we were very soon running into a respectable gale. Yet there was a list, and he reached for it. Mine was the only name entered against this particular cabin number.

'Maybe she didn't fancy paying,' he observed tolerantly. And then someone was calling for him, and he could only advise me either to urge the interloper out or put up with her. 'Maybe you'll be glad of the company as it's going to be such a dirty crossing and another human soul won't come amiss … '

I made my way back to the cabin half hoping that the woman would by now have taken herself off elsewhere. Instead, worse was to come. She had installed herself in the lower bunk and was lying on her back snoring loudly. I could not bring myself to wake her, yet something had to be done. And then the boat gave a violent lurch and I was flung against the wash basin. If I didn't get off my feet I would probably soon have a few broken bones. Seething with impotent fury, I clambered onto the upper berth, where the ceiling seemed uncomfortably close to my head.

My thoughts soon resurrected another occasion on which I had suffered from a chronic snorer. This was the first night I slept with Mademoiselle Haute and was quite one of the most horrible incidents of my childhood. I felt myself go cold at the memory of it. Mature adults do not normally devote much time to pitying themselves in retrospect, yet the effects of some youthful experiences can be lasting. Didn't Darwin once remark that the impulse of the voice is to call for help? Alas, on that occasion, I had no voice. The setting of my first meeting with Mademoiselle Haute was incongruously bright by comparison with the darkness in my soul – the light, chintzy drawing room with french windows looking out onto a sunny garden. There were present my pretty mother, my handsome father and a young man whom I called Jerkey. And there was Mademoiselle Haute, who had just arrived. I thought her the ugliest person I had ever seen. Much to everyone's embarrassment, I refused to have anything to do with her. I covered my ears with my hands when she tried to talk to me. In the end she succeeded in bathing me and seemed delighted with my pink, plump body and flaxen curls.

Once in bed with my favourite doll, I fell deeply asleep; but only for a few hours. When I awoke she was in the bed next to mine, letting forth a veritable cacophony of sound with each intake and release of breath. I tried covering my ears with a pillow, but all to no avail. Finally, I could stand it no longer. I tiptoed over to the communicating door between the nursery and my parents' bedroom and clambered into their bed, begging to be allowed to stay. They said I could do no such thing. My father picked me up and carried me back to my own room. I screamed and fought him like a pole-cat. He reached for a clothes brush and smacked me sharply with it on my bare buttocks. Sobbing at the humiliation, I acknowledged defeat.

By this time Mademoiselle Haute was awake. She wore a white nightgown and a calico sleeping cap. She was at once apologetic and indignant. If she snored – which she did not admit – I must simply roll her over onto her left side.

In the morning I refused to speak to Mademoiselle Haute or to eat my breakfast. Presently, my mother called me into the drawing room for a heart-to-heart talk. Mademoiselle Haute was a Belgian refugee. With the advance of the Germans she and thousands like her had been obliged to flee, leaving all their money and possessions behind. (No money? I pouted my disbelief. She had several golden sovereigns in a little bag. I had seen them and been allowed to touch them.) Taking her in as a governess was just doing *our small bit*. I for my part must be kind and nice to her. And I needed a governess. I scoffed at the very idea. If I needed someone to look after me, couldn't it be Mair, our voluble, disorganised, large-bosomed cook?

'Of course not. Mair couldn't *teach* you anything.'

'But will it be for long?'

It might be. Who could say how long the War might last or what the Kaiser might decide to do next? But couldn't she go somewhere else? Couldn't some other family 'do their bit'? That was ignoble. True, Mademoiselle had mentioned some distant relatives in Wales but that was not the point. To enquire about them or their whereabouts would suggest a lack of generosity on our part. And so I was condemned to a period of the blackest misery I had known before or since, so that my eyes actually brimmed with tears of sympathy for the small helpless creature I had once been.

How strange is the unconscious process of remembering. Not having thought about the incident for years it was now distinct in every detail; and then it was gone, as finally as if a dark curtain had been drawn across my consciousness, buried once again in the limbo of the mind's rejection area.

It was very quiet in the cabin now. The turbulence of the sea seemed to have subsided. I realised that the steamer had docked. Cautiously, I opened the cabin door. A steward was going the rounds with two jugs of tea, one with sugar added and one without. He handed me a mug and I wondered whether he was going to offer my companion some refreshment. He did not do so and then I realised that she was no longer there.

On deck, a striking scenic display greeted the battered troop of passengers. Massive cloud banks all but blacked out the watery onset of the dawn. We soon learned that there had been a landslide on the railway. Inevitably, this meant some delay. The station cafeteria was closed but it seemed there was a guest house nearby where it might be possible to get a pot of tea. I rang the bell several times. At last a woman wearing a red dressing gown with her hair in curlers pulled back the bolts. Naturally, she was surprised to see a lone caller in the hour before dawn.

'I'll get you something,' she agreed, 'Just go into the lounge and wait.'

The lounge was ghostly in its dimness and had a stale, sour odour, yet it was at least somewhere to sit down. I settled myself on the sofa and closed my eyes, taking up the situation again between Mademoiselle Haute and myself. She did not bear me any ill will for my intransigence and appeared to idolise me, despite my sulks. Her attempts to teach me French were rudimentary. Instead, she told me long-winded stories of her childhood in a rough Flemish accent little of which meant anything to me.

I hoped the tea would not be too long in coming. It was a relief to see the door open but alas it was not the proprietor of the guesthouse but my unwelcome companion of the journey. She sat down beside me on the settee. I turned my head away and could only hope that she would take the hint. Obviously, she had not ordered tea as the tray, when it arrived, was only set for one. I drank down the hot, strong, liquid, barely able to conceal my annoyance and, when I had finished, closed my eyes to exclude her from the range of my vision; yet there was not much peace behind the curtain of my closed eyelids. I seemed to be aware of tensions all around me. In the outside world disturbing things were about to happen. I understood them now, even if at the time they posed only a half realised threat. The territory under British jurisdiction was already seen as an almost hopeless security risk. Resistance grew as the Sinn Fein movement spread like an underground fire. Thus, the smiling faces, the warm welcome and the 'blarney' talk had a bitter core, like a rosy apple concealing a maggot, and that accounted even for my beloved Mair. We were in a country ostensibly loyal and co-operative to the national war effort yet at the same time blunderingly, grindingly rebellious. The situation had its effect on all of us. Mademoiselle Haute often complained bitterly to Mair that her life could never be rebuilt. If it were not for *me* she could scarcely have supported her existence in this grim backwater. And Mair would air her views to Mademoiselle Haute on the future, if any, of the British rôle in Ireland. My parents would not have approved of this, had they known about it, yet there was another topic for debate between the two women, and that concerned Jerkey. He seemed to be calling on us nearly every day.

'It's a disgrace for a married woman. In my country ... Why doesn't her husband ... ?'

And Mair: 'Och, true enough it's against the will of God and our Lady ... '

I listened with only half my attention as they rambled on, working themselves up in a fever of resentment against someone who had done them no harm. Mair made excuses to listen outside the drawing room door and report back. As for myself, although I had once adored Jerkey and pestered him to lead me around the garden on my donkey, I began to say rude things to him such as: 'Why do you come here so often? Mademoiselle Haute says you ought to be ashamed of yourself.' And once, when he tried to pick me up to ride on his shoulder, I actually kicked him in the shins.

I opened my eyes to see the owner of the guesthouse bending over me.

'You dropped off,' she said, 'and no wonder. But there's a bus ready now to take passengers to the other side of the land-fall.'

Eagerly, I shook myself out of sleep. I could not get away from the dark, stale smelling room too quickly. I paid for the tea and hurried out into the street. Already the bus was over full. People were complaining, demanding to know when we might make the connection. I tripped over cases and people's feet. At last I found a seat next to a man who looked as exhausted as I was myself. He introduced himself as Peter Ingham, local historian and botanist.

'Where are *you* making for?' he enquired, conversationally.

I explained that I was on my way to stay at a small hotel in a remote spot, Plas Bartroc, which had been specially recommended to me as being out of the ordinary. He said he had heard about this particular house. It had been the family home of a very old lady aged nearly one hundred years old, of Belgian nationality. She had died quite recently and now a young and very enterprising couple had purchased the place for a song and were taking in paying guests. He had a good deal to say about the neighbourhood but suddenly he nodded off into a doze, leaning heavily against my shoulder so that I was pinioned into a most uncomfortable position, which made it difficult to look out of the window at the spectacularly beautiful scenery. The clouds had been rolled back as though by a mighty invisible hand.

The amazing thing was that Mair and Mademoiselle Haute did not seem to realise the dangerous game they were playing. Whispering, eavesdropping, looking through key-holes built up a situation which could not be indefinitely contained, if only on account of my growing hostility to Jerkey. In the end, my mother took me to task about it. My father was away and had arranged for us to drive out in a jaunty-car to a small village on the edge of an enormous sandy beach.

'What *is* all this?' she demanded, as we clopped-clopped along at a leisurely pace. 'Why are you so rude to Jerkey? Someone who had been so kind to you? And you used to adore him.'

I clamped my lips together, and covered my ears with my hands.

'Now, come along, what *is* it?'

And then I blurted it all out. What Mademoiselle Haute and Mair said to each other, about them listening at doors, and so on. It was quite a long speech for me for I was not as a rule a talkative child and gradually my volubility petered into silence. I glanced at my mother covertly. The expression on her face struck cold terror into my heart. Her jaw was taut and her eyes like agate. She broke our mutual silence only once to tell the coachman to turn round and head for home. As soon as we arrived, she sent me straight to the nursery and ordered me to stay there. Then she sent a message by Mair to request Mademoiselle Haute to come to the drawing room within half an hour. My father was due home later that evening and my parents were going out to dinner. My mother emerged from her bedroom, resplendent in evening dress. Mademoiselle Haute went to her doom cheerfully, having no idea of what lay in store for her. Mair and I converged on the hall where through the closed door we could hear their rising voices.

'And I am amazed, Mademoiselle, horrified, that you should repay my kindness in this way. As soon as I can make arrangements for you to go to another family you will be out of this house. And I hope that will be *tomorrow*.'

Mademoiselle Haute broke into a litany of pleading and self-justification. She begged not to be humiliated and exposed to universal condemnation but the nub of it was that she could not bear to be parted from *me*; but it was all to no avail.

At last she emerged from the drawing room, a crushed, broken figure, and dragged herself up the stairs to the nursery. As for myself, I was too shattered to realise my good fortune in being rid of her, for there would not be much pleasure in my life unless my mother restored me to her favour.

How strange is the atrophying of emotion. I must have been as unhappy as any child living that evening after my parents left for their dinner party: with Mair retreating to the kitchen and Mademoiselle Haute swinging aimlessly to and fro in the nursery rocking chair. Yet now nothing of it remained, except for disconnected flashbacks.

I opened my eyes as the bus collided violently with a high bank. Below, was a precipice, too close for comfort. All around me, people were asking how far we were from the railway line. And then, when I had thought we were free of her, the wretched woman who had dogged me throughout my journey was around again. There was no room for her anywhere in the crowded upturned bus and so she had perched herself on the arm of my seat. True, she did not exert any pressure, yet her intrusion was really quite intolerable.

The front wheels of the coach were sunk deep in the ditch, the nose of the engine half buried. When everyone had scrambled out of the emergency door the general feeling was that we were lucky to be alive. At first, we all talked in rather high-pitched voices, displaying a courage we did not feel but soon this gave way to the consideration of what to do next.

The driver, though shaken, was unhurt: 'I could get to the nearest village,' he suggested, 'and telephone for a breakdown van and another coach and then that would get you all to the nearest railway station.'

He was rewarded by a chorus of grateful thanks. Yet, obviously it was going to take some hours, even the whole day! Peter Ingham explained that as a veteran hiker he always had a large-scale map with him. He produced it now and spread it out on the grass for me to study.

'Look', he said, 'We're not more than a couple of miles as the crow flies to Plas Bartroc. It would be quicker to walk.'

'Walk?' I considered the route with misgivings. True, I could see that Bartroc seemed only a short distance away but such indications on a map can be very misleading. We were in brown tinted territory which meant high hills. The house, Plas Bartroc, was in a green area so at some point we would need to make a descent. There was no sign of a road although at some points a dotted line indicated a footpath.

'We could be there within an hour,' he promised eagerly. 'Save all this hanging about and I do assure you you won't see the country a better way.'

So I agreed, for if we could manage it, it made sense. Fortunately, I had learned to travel with the very minimum of luggage. My bag could, he explained, be strapped onto my shoulders. 'That way, it takes the strain.'

Who was it who had said that? It was not his voice, which had a bell-like tone, but one hoarse and unfamiliar. I looked around, but there was no one close to us.

'Are you ready?' he asked, 'Then we may as well get going.'

How right he had been! The track was an old drovers' way, still used by shepherds. It followed the spine of the hill with on either side a truly magnificent panorama. On our left was a steep drop to the valley and on the right a stark bastion of rock casting perpetual shadow of grey and mauve. The sun shone. The sky was clear, and because of the pristine atmosphere I felt exhilarated.

'It won't be long now. The time will pass quickly.'

The words were quite distinct, yet again, it did not sound like his voice. He was some paces ahead and the distance must have distorted the vibrations. We glimpsed red squirrels: once, a hawk; there were rabbits untroubled by myxomatosis and an adder coiled on a hot slab of stone. I stared at it in horror for I had always had an unreasoning fear of snakes. At one point our way was blocked by a waterfall, cascading from a great height, the water frothing at its base; a place of natural beauty, as yet mercifully free of toilets, kiosks and the inevitable car-park. It was memorably, poignantly beautiful. Yet that said, the distance really did seem rather longer than he had indicated. We had to climb an almost vertical hillside and the path was now virtually non-existent. Annoyingly, I began panting and gasping for breath. At last, I said I must rest and Peter Ingham wandered off in search of plant specimens, leaving me to enjoy the view; yet I saw little of it for my vision was almost completely blurred by fatigue and behind my closed eyelids other images gradually materialised.

I was being unceremoniously aroused from sleep and dragged protesting along a path which led to the railway station. The platform was thronged by women wearing long black shawls over their heads. They swayed in a kind of unselfconscious rhythm while a strange, haunting chant welled up from their throats. They were 'keening' a farewell to their men as they left for the 'front' and as the train pulled out they ran along side it, clutching at the doors, weeping; and I wept too, struggling to free myself, crushed under her weight while she tied her scarf over my mouth to quieten me.

On the boat she tried to reassure me. 'You will be so happy where we are going. Mademoiselle will take you to a beautiful place and we will live there together with no one to make things cruel or try to part us ... ' But of course, I was not so easily consoled.

When I opened my eyes Peter Ingham was sitting beside me and suggested that we might now go on. He spread out the map and showed me again how big a detour we would have been making if we had taken the ordinary travel route. He seemed very anxious that I should be convinced and to please him I agreed. In any case, it was the truth. Plas Bartroc must lie folded away on the other side of the next summit. And so indeed it might, yet I insisted that I must rest for at least a little longer.

I was on the boat once again. It was crowded to the point of suffocation. People pressed against us, talking and gesticulating. Something terrible had occurred in Dublin. The 'Volunteers', assisted by the 'Citizen' army, had paraded through the city streets and occupied the main Post Office in O'Connell Street. Shots had been fired and hundreds of prisoners rounded up. Kilmashogue had been 'taken'. St Stephen's Green was 'occupied' by the 'Countess' and her troops – or soon would be. Anti-British feeling ran dangerously high. The Germans were the new allies, the English the doers of all evil.

'To be away from all that – that is something,' Mademoiselle murmured sentiously. 'We must put trust in Our Lady while such evil forces are let loose.'

The sea had been choppy when we embarked but as we moved out into the open waters we ran into a minor hurricane. The steamer pitched and rocked alarmingly. Waves, many feet high, hemmed us in between grey-green walls. People were flung from side to side, their political affiliations forgotten. The smell of nausea, the screams and impact of heavy bodies had the worst possible effect on me and soon I became a victim of an almost lethal sea-sickness. Eventually, I was carried ashore, still retching although there was no food left in my exhausted stomach. Alarmed by my condition Mademoiselle Haute took me to a hotel and booked a room for a few hours. There I lay supine in a vast cavern of a room while she went to make arrangements for the remainder of our journey. Once left alone, with some barley water to sip, I began to recover and, bored with my own company, crept to the door and looked out into the corridor. It was dimly lit, and the regiments of closed doors scared me so much that I hastened back into the bed.

Soon, Mademoiselle Haute reappeared. 'Just imagine,' she said, 'We are travelling by horse and cart. There is no railway anywhere near to where we are going and you will so much enjoy the drive.'

She was over-optimistic. Daylight did not rest kindly on the decrepit dog-cart and emaciated horse. We clip-clopped through the streets and soon emerged into the open countryside. I lay on the floor, covered by a rug, refusing to look out at what she assured me was a wonderful landscape. Once or twice she and the driver stopped for food and drink but I refused to join them. The road became tortuous and the horse advanced slowly with a slightly uneven gait. We were climbing, that much was obvious even to me, and once I peeped out from under the rug to glimpse what seemed to me a very high mountain. And then suddenly I was thrown forward by a violent jolt. We came to a halt. The horse was down on one fore-leg, with the shafts pressing cruelly into his flank. The coachman admonished, tugged at the reins, swore, lashed with his whip. I cried out to him to stop. It was all to no avail and at last the man, red faced and sweating, acknowledged defeat. The horse had gone completely lame.

'I can't shift it, missus. A stone, right deep in his hoof. Only a smithy can get it out.'

'But you promised,' Mademoiselle Haute cried angrily. 'You gave me your word. I paid you.'

He did not offer to return her money. 'Only thing you can do is to walk it, if you mean to get there before dark. If the little one can manage it, that is. Not above a half hour I'd say, if you go right over the top of Ben Bartroc.'

And so we set off on foot along a tortuous ever mounting track while she half-carried, half dragged me and I begged vainly for rest and a drink of water.

My companion returned from his explorations.

'How are you now? Do you feel rested? Do you think we could go on now? It's really not very far once we get to the top of Ben Bartroc.'

Clearly, he felt guilty. Being so accustomed to climbing and walking, it had not occurred to him that everyone might not feel the same. Of course I agreed. We could not go back so must press on! But for me there was no pleasure in it. I felt resentful as though he had done me some wrong. And the way certainly became rougher. We walked single file now along a tortuous trail, hemmed in on either side by a sheer rock face. And then, as we rounded a corner of the mountain, I saw something which really angered me. That wretched woman was in front of us, gesticulating wildly, urging us forward. She must have taken a detour and somehow got ahead of us. I whispered to Peter Ingham not to get involved. He glanced at me anxiously, but did not reply. And so we continued, the three of us, in uneasy silence.

'We're almost there,' he assured me. 'Once we get to the top you'll see Plas Bartroc.'

He assisted me over a pyramid of boulders. Our footsteps released an avalanche of stones. Yet the woman leapt over them without assistance. Once at the summit it was some moments before I could concentrate on the scene immediately ahead. When I did so I was silenced by its sheer, unspoiled beauty. Plas Bartroc was a jewel set in enveloping parkland: fronted by a lake and backed by a wood. It was an unusually compact almost continental structure of at least four storeys with pointed gables decorated in the Belgian style. It would have captured any visitor's attention. As for me, I stood transfixed for *it was the house of my dream*.

And yet – not quite. It was very much smaller and seemed to be facing a different way. The steps were not steep and there were only two of them. These gnarled and mis-shapen trees, one of which resembled a coiled boa-constrictor, were surely never in my dream. I felt confused and disorientated and somehow cheated by the discrepancies between what I had imagined and the actual building in front of me.

Meanwhile, Peter Ingham had gone forward to seek out the proprietors, to tell them that I had arrived and to reserve a room for himself. He did not refer to our unwelcome companion, but at all costs *she* must not be allowed to book in with us, and I was prepared to tell her so, but when I looked around for her she had disappeared.

Barry and Hayley Stuart-Wyn, the young couple running the place, were glad to see us. The sun shone and they were optimistic about the future of their venture.

'Once people know how marvellous it is here at Bartroc they'll want to come. Who wants to live in a city again? *We* don't.' Hayley explained that they served only health foods – home-baked bread and compost-grown vegetables – taken care of by Barry. Their faces shone with enthusiasm and they were hard to resist. My bedroom was magnificent, overlooking the lake. How had such an elaborate building programme ever been carried out in the fastness of the Welsh hills? Navvy labour, no doubt, alas, for Plas Bartroc had been built in the uncaring mid-eighteen hundreds by a rich Belgian merchant who had made his money exporting jute and timber from Dundee. Hayley and Barry had decorated the bedrooms and the corridors with white paint yet strangely, to me, the entire interior was in shadow, even though the evening was still several hours away.

When at last dusk descended the lake became a vast opaque arena; the water still as a sheet of black glass, disturbed only from time to time by a translucent, floating object which might have been the flower of a water plant. Presently, a bell summoned us to dinner. The thought came to me that the woman might by now have reappeared. It would be disastrous if she insisted on sitting with me; but when I entered the dining room I saw that the guests were all at one large polished table, lit by candles. Because the day had been so warm the windows were still open and the lake seemed like an extension of the room.

The guests were all pleasant, easy-going people, some

touring, others staying at Plas Bartroc for the walking and vegetarian diet. I could not help thinking how out of place the woman would have been, with her outlandish dress and long-winded utterances. But where was she? Plas Bartroc was the only house within miles. As Hayley served me with a delicious nut roast on a bed of green vegetables, I enquired casually whether anyone else had booked in with me and Mr Ingham?

'Oh, no', Hayley replied blithely, 'We are completely full up tonight. Later on, we shall have an annexe in the garden but it's not ready yet.'

So what a relief. Yet as I entered into a long discussion with a couple from Minnesota I was still wondering about her. Could she possibly have collapsed from exhaustion? Was she even now lying semi-conscious somewhere in the gathering darkness?

I went out onto the terrace and peered into the curiously pale twilight. I followed a gravel path which led to an enclosed lawn. There was no sign of a prostrate figure and I continued on towards the park. The moon was rising. Sheep moved like phantoms against the impenetrable darkness of the wood. I was glad to return to the house. The dining room was empty now, and I stood looking out at the lake while I considered the strangeness of the situation. Suddenly, I heard a loud splash. Something floated on the surface, so briefly as to be an illusion, for it resembled an upturned face. I turned back into the room, groping my way towards the door, feeling quite ill with horror at what I had seen. And then a strange phenomenon occurred. It was like watching a film with anticipation and interest until, almost at the end, one episode seems familiar. You have seen the film before, yet the recollection of it was not retained. That is what happened to me at that moment. I *had* been in this house and this room. I was crying: hauled by Mademoiselle Haute up the steps and into the room by the french windows. There were figures at the far end: a youngish person not known to me; a man wearing an old-fashioned Norfolk jacket and a smart, beautiful woman in Edwardian dress whom I recognised at my parents; and a uniformed police officer. They advanced towards us. Their lips moved, but I could not hear what they said. Mademoiselle Haute let go my arm. She gave a loud cry and ran towards the parapet. There was a sickening impact as her body hit the water. Everyone rushed forward, but it was too late. She had vanished, except for one fleeting, hideous moment when her face surfaced, like a floating plate. The police officer and my father dived into the lake, but darkness hampered their search through what remained of that terrible night.

Next morning, my enquiries must have sounded rather implausible and I made them tentatively. I would not have wished to reveal a long-ago tragedy at Plas Bartroc to Hayley and Barry. In any case, they were not able to tell me very much about the house's past history.

'In the deeds,' Barry explained, 'There were only two owners; the man who built Plas Bartroc in 1866 and his niece, the ninety-year old lady who died about two years ago, leaving this place derelict.'

There, it seemed, I would have to leave it, even allowing that I might have been suffering from hallucinations. I wandered around the parkland in a vain hope of some reassurance until at last Mr Ingham sought me out in the orchard and persuaded me to tell him what was wrong, for he seemed grieved that apparently I was not appreciating the unique amenities of Plas Bartroc. On impulse I told him the whole strange sequence of my experiences since leaving Ireland.

'I expect you'll think I'm mad but it's all been so extraordinarily real.'

'No, no,' he protested. 'These weird things do happen when one least expects them. I once had a similar kind of visitation myself. It was to do with a boy at my school who was drowned in a boating accident ... It's something we should clear up if we possibly can.'

He made a practical suggestion: 'I've often found that the local churchyard provides most of the answers. If the woman's grave is here at Bartroc ... well, that would be a kind of confirmation.'

I agreed, and we set off across the park to Bartroc church. Peter Ingham explained that we might not find conditions similar to an ordinary English country parish church.

Although centuries ago the Welsh Church had been merged into the Church of England the strong dissident movements meant that it had never taken a real hold.

'You don't get the 'cosy' atmosphere of the English vicarage, with a kindly, silver-haired vicar waiting to welcome the casual caller ... '

I assured him that I understood perfectly, that it was not important for I had by now convinced myself that we would find Mademoiselle Haute's grave in the Bartroc cemetery. Yet I was doomed to disappointment. The little graveyard wore an even more desolate air than the most run-down of its English counterparts. Apart from a small cluster of raw, new graves, no others were visible, except for a few humps in the long grass. Wind sighed in the trees, rooks cawed, a light breeze sprang up, yet there was no real life in the place, or ever would be.

Seeing how cast down I was, Peter Ingham had one more suggestion to make; that we should attempt to inspect the parish register. Even more than headstones, these records sometimes yielded up hidden truths. He went in search of someone who might be willing to unlock the vestry and show us the register. I sat on that part of the surrounding wall which remained intact, facing the valley, yet I saw nothing of it. The shutter which had slid back so briefly remained open. I was back in the cheerful drawing room at Kobv, and yet a shadow hung over our lives. Perhaps it came from outside as the situation surrounding us became increasingly menacing and intense – or was it from within ourselves? Presently a new drama erupted. My father was summoned from his bed at dawn. A coastguard had spotted a small craft carrying arms and ammunition for the Irish Nationalists. A collapsible dinghy was already on its way towards Tralee. It carried one passenger – Roger Casement.

A few days later it was all over. Leaders imprisoned, marched away, shot. Soon afterwards my father was transferred to a more important assignment. We did not follow him. My mother and I returned to England and my handsome, volatile parents did not occupy the same house again.

Peter Ingham returned, smiling. He had been successful and the Bartroc parish register of births, deaths and marriages was available for our inspection.

We entered the vestry in company with a stooping, very elderly man who explained in a Welsh, lilting voice, that it was one of the oldest in the Kingdom, dating back to the sixteenth century. He opened it at the pages of the year 1915 and ran his fore-finger over the entries. There were very few of them and it looked as though once again we had drawn a blank. And then we saw it: written so faintly in the margin as to be almost undecipherable: 'April 18 1915 Margharette Haute *felo-de-se.*

Although Peter Ingham was as elated as I was myself about this discovery he was equally intrigued by the Parish register itself because, as he explained, so many of these valuable records were now rendered obsolete by an unthinking ecclesiastical decree. This one had entries dating from 1538 and he set about studying them and making notes.

I sat for a few moments in one of the pews, feeling suddenly rather shaky and let down. The little church was airless and very cold, while a pervasive mustiness suggested that it was seldom if ever used for services and ordinary parish activities. Yet that could not always have been so; for I seemed to see a timid yet generous cleric who, despite the rigorous legislation of the age, could not bring himself to let a death go totally unrecorded.

I had much to think about and for a long while I pondered the question. Did she pursue her unreal travel without cease or only when the stars and planets converged propitiously to recreate the conditions of the journey? Or was it my unwitting intrusion on the route that drew forth from an unmarked grave the unquiet spirit of a woman eternally seeking fulfilment and rehabilitation?

How could one ever know?

II

Station Cab

J.C. Trewin

The wire to Hampstead was brief enough: 'Come quickly. Molly worse.' No more. It was signed Lawson, the name of the doctor at Bozawn.

Hugh knew that only urgency could have made him telegraph. The railway time-table was on the bureau. Trains to South Cornwall? ... 'I can just get to Paddington for the three-thirty,' he exclaimed to Molly's sister, Sylvia.

'Perhaps we can telephone to the doctor?' she said anxiously, a little unsure of what these instruments might involve. 'The Lauders have one next door.'

'Can you try while I pack?'

She was back very soon. 'I'm sorry, Hugh; there's no way at all of speaking; they say the lines are down.' The storm that had ravaged the South-West on a winter Wednesday and Thursday of 1902 had not yet reached London in any force, though rain had begun to blur the panes. Hugh's nephew, rushing round Rosslyn Hill for a cab, brought back with him the *Pall Mall Gazette.* Hugh glanced at it before he made his good-byes and then while the old horse trotted towards Paddington.

Devon and Cornwall, he gathered from a fervent description, were still in chaos: all the customary trouble, roads and fields flooded, trees uprooted, bridges impassable, houses unroofed, the gale unabated. He had hardly taken it in before the cab was swishing down an incline to the terminus. His work in London was cut off halfway, but he could trust

Sylvia to leave the right messages, and nothing mattered now but to get home, and as swiftly as he could. Sylvia would be wiring to Bozawn.

Paddington was certainly under the weather. Barely a dozen people, all a trifle distrait, were at the booking-office. Rain was pouring now.

'Single to Gwavas,' he asked. 'Can I get through?'

'Well, you never know, sir,' the clerk said cheerfully, rather too cheerfully. 'It may be a long haul.'

It was. Alone in his third-class compartment, his small bag on the opposite seat, he sat in an impatient fret which increased as the train moved glumly westward in the twilight and December gloom. Few were travelling, and for some reason this jarred on Hugh: talk, he thought, might have helped him. It was a poor train; they had to go round by Bristol which lengthened a journey already trying. Hugh began without success to remember the paper-work he had left unfinished. Useless: he could think of nothing but Molly who had been happily convalescent when he left her – only for three days, he had said to her acquiescent doctor. Now this unexpected relapse. She would be looked after, he knew – Ethel and Florrie could not be kinder – but anxiety had possessed him.

It was scarcely allayed by the train's behaviour, crawling, hesitating, stopping, as it entered what the *Pall Mall*, crushed under his seat, had called 'the areas of danger'. The sea, scourged by a formidable wind, was high and granite-grey, and the rain pelting, as they loitered along the Devon coast; Dawlish and Teignmouth had never looked less inviting. With the gale unabated, and battering against the oil-lamps that swung on every deserted country station, they came in their own good time to Hemerdon and at length put on a welcome speed as they ran down towards Plymouth.

The estuary of the Plym, usually a placid mirror, had swirled over its banks by Laira; Hugh could not see the wintry woods of Saltram across the way. Mutley station was dim beyond the tunnel; then, almost adjoining, they were at Plymouth North Road, certainly two hours late, perhaps more, and a bunch of railwaymen on the platform with nothing in particular to say about anything.

Hugh would remember little of the ensuing journey through Cornwall once they were beyond Saltash Bridge which that night had seemed to him as adventurous a passage as Blondin's above the falls of Niagara. A furious wind appeared to impel them towards the south. Very late – he could not recall when, though he had a dim recollection of Camborne – he was the sole passenger to get out at Carn Nance for the brief branch-line run to Gwavas. By then – his unwound watch had stopped – it must have been well past midnight. To his astonishment a train was there, steam up, ready to take him, its sole client, over the suddenly flat, unsheltered miles towards Gwavas, an area where one of the train's ancestors had been snowed up in the Great Blizzard of 1891.

'A rare old buster!' affirmed the guard, a remote, bearded figure in his dripping oilskins, 'but we'll get 'ee there, sir.'

They did in about twenty-five minutes. Hugh handed his ticket to a collector whom he recognised vaguely as an old acquaintance, but who, dumb tonight, could only nod wanly as Hugh emerged into the concentrated storm that was Gwavas station yard. He had still eleven miles before him; Bozawn, as he had often been told, was at the end of everything. How exactly he would cover those miles in a rare old buster he had hardly dared to ask himself.

The station yard could scarcely have been wetter or have looked emptier. Not a light flickered in the houses that he knew were behind the station approach; for a moment he wondered whether the houses were really there. The cobbled road was like a growing lake, one of the 'areas of danger', no doubt, though the *Pall Mall* could not have inspected it.

It was utterly absurd to dream of finding any vehicle that night. The Bozawn horse-bus would have lumbered off many hours before, and it was plain that nothing else would venture on the journey. Well, what was the answer? Should he try to knock up the Pellowes at the Gwavas Inn? Should he get back to the indifferent shelter of the station? No, he had to go on, he told himself stoutly; if needed he would walk, though heaven only knew how such a vow could be kept.

Wildly, he believed he saw a tiny glimmer about fifty yards down the road. Nonsense, yet when he looked again it was still there. Struggling up to it, he saw to his amazement that it was – it could not have been, but it was – a cab, a primitive affair, oscillating violently as the gusts struck at it. Beside it Hugh sensed, rather than saw, a tall man muffled in a top-coat, layers of them it seemed, with a great hat jammed down over his forehead so that his face was practically invisible. What Hugh could see in the lantern's candle-glimmer looked oddly bleached; still, nobody could be sure in this rain and darkness. He was stroking with a gloved hand the bay mare that stood, drenched, between the shafts, holding herself steady against the unrelenting wind. (Hugh wondered why those new Gwavas houses on the hill did not give more protection.)

'Dreadful night!' he said and realised, as he spoke, how absurd this sounded.

The man did not stir.

'Can you take me to Bozawn, I wonder? ... It's urgent, a matter of illness.' No response; Hugh might not have been there, but he went on: 'I don't know what your fare is ... I'll pay you double or treble if you can get me there tonight' (or should he have said 'morning'?).

The words were tumbling out. Still no sign of a reply. Staring at the cab, Hugh could discern very dimly something that might have been a coat-of-arms painted on a side panel, one that had been crumpled, jagged across, as by a heavy blow. It could be a private cab, he supposed, though for the life of him he could not see where the owner might be coming from in this ghastly night. Or, for that matter, where he would be going.

Now, with no hint at all that he had heard anything Hugh had said, this most taciturn of drivers tugged open the cab door and motioned to him to enter. Scarcely able to credit his luck, he threw his bag inside, collapsing on the seat as the wind – which blew, it appeared, from the north-west – struck once more at the cab and caused it to vibrate again on its solid wheels. When Hugh had collected himself, the man had already mounted to his driving seat and the vehicle was lurching round to the long descent from the station and what should normally have been the Gwavas main street with a family memorial at its foot.

It was clear that the windows were not made to open. Hugh

felt that he was caught up in a roomy sack, enveloped in a coarse, clinging smell – mildew, no doubt – from the fraying leather with which the cab was lined. Not that he speculated. He was only too relieved to be in some sort of conveyance. This one was moving slowly, far too slowly; in the turmoil of the night he presumed that was inevitable.

Other things had begun to puzzle Hugh. The road to Bozawn, as he recalled it, and after all he had been over it hundreds of times, was reasonably well metalled and frequently inspected. Yet the cab seemed now to be struggling through a perilous, heavily-rutted narrow lane. And how had they left the town behind so swiftly? Though Hugh could distinguish little except amorphous shapes, he knew the area well; he could not tell himself why, within a couple of minutes or less, they were buffeting on between unclipped hedges when they should have been in the main street of Gwavas, its shops as familiar to him as the view from his window at home.

Probably, he decided, it was a fresh route, even if he could not fathom how the driver had discovered anything fresh on a journey so direct. Pressing his face against the dirty pane, he waited for what he knew must be the cross-roads hamlet of Penleath, with its Griffin Inn, a mile southward. Nothing whatever came; and a hundred yards or so past where Penleath should have been, and where Hugh recalled the beginning of a messy group of modern villas – he had complained about them himself – not a brick showed. Indeed, on either side, he made out in the darkness nothing but an apparent fringe of bare moorland. Seeking to solve the puzzle, he tried to call the driver, but in this tempest it was a waste of time and he resigned himself. The man must somehow know better than he did himself; in any event they were heading in the right direction, much too slowly but (so he believed) on the way.

At that point he was aware that they were moving steadily downhill. It could be one place only, Poldine Valley, the single dip in the road to Bozawn. Immediately as Hugh had decided upon this, the cab lurched to a halt that shook him to the floor. The driver had got out to push wide a pair of ornamental iron gates on the right of the road – a country lane that should have been twice the width. Next they turned in sharply and were pounding through what was obviously a private drive where leafless branches swayed desperately over the thickets.

Hugh was seriously disturbed. Had the man got it wrong? Why choose a private by-road? If this was what he thought, it would be impossible to get through; the one place it could be between Gwavas and Bozawn was the empty mansion of the Carne family behind which the fields stretched, roadless, to the sea.

The Carnes had owned Poldine House across many generations. On old Sir Franklin's death it had been left vacant for years; Hugh had heard that somebody in a Tasmanian branch to which it had descended was coming to live there. He was recalling this when their wheels ground on a wide sweep of gravel; behind it lights glowed in the first-floor windows of an unseen facade. The cab turned one corner and a second, and stopped beneath a wooden canopy outside what must have been the kitchens. For a minute the small space was eerily quiet; the driver stood where lamplight filled an open door and an elderly mob-capped woman, a servant no doubt, greeted him. They vanished together within the house.

Hugh sat on angrily, asking himself why a man he had hired on urgent business should have made this preposterous and unexplained detour; he attempted to shout, but the words would not form. The wait must have lasted some time. When the driver and the woman reappeared, the man was carrying a pewter mug and Hugh heard the woman say (the only words he seemed to have heard in a lifetime) 'This do for you, Dick?' The man nodded, drank, handed the mug back, and mounted to his place. The cab swerved round while the woman waved and they were out presently on the gravel, passing the lighted windows – maybe the new Carnes had come at last – and exposed to the full diapason of the storm.

Through the iron gates; sharp right to what must have been that shrunken main road. In the teeming rain the bay mare clopped on even slower than before. They climbed from the Poldine valley. Mile by mile they toiled due south. Then of a sudden the gale snatched at a toppling stunted elm by the granite hedge, tore it from its insecure roots, and tossed it with such force that it struck the cab's side-panel beneath the right-hand window.

They hurtled across the road to the opposite rim; Hugh realised in a terrified flash that below them was a sheer plunge into Carne quarry. Through a lull before the next gust he heard a horse whinny and a man's high-pitched shriek that dwindled into nothing as the gale thrust it away.

At the last second the cab seemed to right itself and to swing back on its course. How, Hugh was thinking – how could the place have been left unfenced, the most dangerous within miles? Yet, even as he asked himself, he knew that here since his boyhood there had been a high wall sturdily reinforced. The cab had thudded on while he sat shivering; now, as it were beneath the wind, he was conscious of a clatter of hooves and two or three shadowy horsemen, scarcely glimpsed as they galloped by his right-hand window into the blackness ahead. From somewhere a line slipped into his mind: 'I did hear the galloping of horse. Who was't came by?'

Who came by? ... Starting up from a daze that could have been endless, he was aware that the cab had stopped and that the door was open. Clumsily he stumbled out into the gale. Beside him, still speechless, the driver waited.

'But this is not Bozawn!' Hugh exclaimed.

The driver pointed to his left. By the thin glimmer of the cab lantern, Hugh traced the outline of a granite cross embedded in the hedge. There was a similar cross beside the Green at Bozawn, but surely that stood upright, moved he could not say how many years since? Yet why was he worrying about dates? The driver had extended his arm, and Hugh, fumbling sleepily, dropped two sovereigns into a hand that, without its glove, was bleached and bloodless.

'Thank you,' he muttered. 'Where should I have been without your help?' The man paid no heed. Dumbly as ever, he seized the reins. The cab with its gashed panel and its single glimmering light moved off into the gloom.

Hugh put out a hand towards the cross in the hedge; he felt its rough, serrated surface; then darkness called to darkness and he fainted clean away.

*

A firm hand on his shoulder roused him. 'What's wrong, Mr Hugh?'

He clambered stiffly to his feet. It was grey morning now. The rare buster had blown itself out and the rain had eased to a drizzle. Lights were springing up round the Green; Hugh heard the distant lowing of cattle.

Peter Lyne, the South Farm's veteran, stood watching him. 'What happened, then?'

'I'm quite all right, Peter. Faint, I daresay. Anyway, it's over now.'

'Over! Well, you'm drenched. And how did 'ee get here? Not walked from Gwavas, I'll warrant ... Look now, what's that by you?'

They looked down. Beside Hugh's feet and his soaked bag two sovereigns glittered on the turf.

Bewildered, he bent to them. 'That was my fare, Peter.'

'A pretty night's work, Mr Hugh. And who earned it, may I ask?'

Hugh saw that the cross was upright upon the hedge as it had been since his childhood. He glanced up the way he must have come, that broad, straight road from the north. Wearily, he tried to explain.

The old man was silent. Then: 'I wouldn't ha' been in your place, Mr Hugh. You were riding with Dick Trevellick.'

'Dick Trevellick?'

'Not a name you'd know, I'd say. He worked full forty years for the Carnes at Poldine, labouring and hedging, often far gone in liquor but a man who knew his job. When he left at last they set him up with one of their old carriages – not so much of a carriage either – and he made his bit driving round the villages from Gwavas with his bay mare. He died on a night like this – a tree snapped in a gale on the Upper Moor and he ended in the quarry. Far, far down. They'd sent out ridgers to find him, but 'twas too late. Seventy years ago at least, but they say he's never off the road ... Mr Hugh, you'm white as an apron. I'll see 'ee home.'

It was a half-mile walk to the house above the cove. Neither spoke much. Florrie was out to meet them. 'Thank the Lord ... Doctor's been, Mr Hugh. It's all well; she's better, turned an hour after we wired and slept till morning ... Ah, Peter! Come in and warm yourself. Will you go up, sir?'

She was better indeed. Propped against her pillows, she greeted him thankfully. 'But Hugh,' she said after a while, 'how could you have managed it? Such a night, Florrie tells me, such a storm!'

'No trouble,' he heard himself saying. 'No trouble at all. I took the station cab.'

III

The Saracen's Stick

Fred Urquhart

Cameron was sitting, chin on knees, in an embrasure of one of the three remaining towers of the ruined castle, gazing out to sea, when he saw Mr Hikmet waddle through the great archway into the courtyard. Knowing the fat Turk had not seen him yet, Cameron slipped down and crouched behind some fallen masonry.

A voice behind him whispered: 'Who are you hiding from?'

A boy of about his own age, eleven, was leaning against the green-tinged stone wall: a boy half-naked like himself, except that Cameron wore brief white shorts and this boy wore a kilted kind of saffron coloured loin cloth. Cameron stared. It was like looking at himself in a mirror – the same cap of short-cut curly scarlet hair, the same white face with an alabastrine sheen, the same height, the same arrogant poise of the head thrusting out from the same slim shoulders.

'Who are you hiding from?' the strange boy repeated.

'From him,' Cameron said. 'That man down there.'

The boy said: 'Why?'

'Because he keeps touching me with his sweaty hands and poking me with his stick,' Cameron said. 'I don't like him.'

'The Emir Sulieman, lord of all he surveys,' the boy said. 'Who could like the Saracen slug?'

'He's not an emir and he's not a Saracen,' Cameron said. 'His name is Hikmet and he's a Turkish millionaire.'

'He is the Emir Sulieman,' the boy said. 'I know him from olden days. I know him far too well, and I have an old score to settle. I'll get rid of him. As soon as I speak to him, run for your life and don't look back.'

Cameron said: 'Who are you?'

'I am a Christian boy called Simon,' he said and vanished.

The next instant he was in the courtyard walking towards the fat Turk. Cameron did not pause to wonder how Simon had reached the courtyard so quickly; he skirted round the masonry and, looking to make sure the Turk's back was to him, he darted down the stairs and into the archway. Once inside the shadow of its thick wall, his curiosity made him look back. He saw Simon dancing in front of the Turk and, walking backwards, lead the man towards the wide stone steps down to the black passages and underground caverns, all that remained of the old Saracen dungeons. The boy kept capering provocatively, and the Turk was waving his stick and laughing.

Cameron ran towards the village, the hotel and safety, wondering who the boy was and how he could have appeared like that out of the air.

* * *

Perhaps if Nanny Cruikshank had remained in the Lebanon Cameron might never have been pestered by the fat Turk or have visited the Saracen's castle. If Nanny had had her way Cameron would have spent the summer in Scotland with his parents. But Sir Ranald Locherbie did not want to interrupt a very delicate diplomatic negotiation in Beirut by going home to Ardavalloch for even a short period. And so Cameron came to the Lebanon instead. Sir Ranald had arranged that one of his prep school teachers would take Cameron to the airport and a stewardess would look after him on the plane. But Sir Ranald had reckoned without Nanny Cruikshank, who had been ruining his plans since he was a boy and whom he thought safely ensconced now, out of reach, as chatelaine of Ardavalloch. Nanny said it was a fair scandal that the poor bairn should be expected to travel all that distance alone into the wilds with only a label round his neck, so to speak. It was a perfect disgrace to the Family, and although she loathed setting foot in a plane she would bring the dear lamb to Beirut herself.

If Sir Ranald had reckoned without Nanny, she had reckoned without the Lebanon heat. 'However do you thole it, Miss Ollie?' she said to Lady Locherbie. 'It's like being in a steaming hot bath-tub. All my undies are sticking to me.'

'You shouldn't wear so many, Nan dear,' Olive said. 'Be like me and wear practically none.'

'Och, I wouldn't feel decent. Just think if I got knocked down and what they'd say at the hospital when they found I hadn't a stitch on except my jumper and skirt. I'd never live it down. And neither, I'm sure, would you nor Sir Ranald either.'

'Well, you'll just have to keep your weather eye open and see you don't get knocked down,' Lady Locherbie said.

Nanny's stay was not long enough, however, for her to keep her weather eye on anything; for she had been only two days in Beirut when Dr Mitchell at Ardavalloch phoned and told her to return to Scotland at the toot because her sister Libby, who had been left to uphold the family name and keep the other estate retainers on their toes, had broken her hip. And so, protesting loudly at the inconvenience and about leaving the Family to cope without her, Nanny set off, in grey twin set, thick grey flannel skirt, thick ankles over-lapping stout sensible black lacing shoes, her apple cheeks wrinkled and her small mouth puckered with self-righteous Scottish disapproval of Middle Eastern dirt and degradation.

Cameron was delighted to see the back of Nanny. So was his father. 'I'm so chuffed to get rid of the old girl, I'm over the moon,' Sir Ranald said. Ranald had endured Nanny's domination ever since his mother had died when he was two years old. Even marriage to Olive had not lessened the domination, for Nanny had taken on a mother-in-law role. Olive, heiress of the neighbouring estate, was an orphan too, and Nanny had taken her under her wing. At Ardavalloch the Locherbies were also under the domineering eye of Libby Cruikshank, who had been the fork to her sister's knife from the time they were born within sixteen months of each other in the head gardener's cottage.

'Sometimes I wonder why some of the other peasants don't do Nanny and Libby in,' Ranald said to his wife when he returned from seeing Nanny off at the airport. 'I could lay a bet on it that some joker is responsible for our Lib's broken hip. What odds'll you give that she wasn't up a ladder keeking into the kitchen maid's bedroom?'

'There are no kitchen maids at Ardavalloch nowadays, darling,' Olive said.

'Well, I mean the equivalent,' he said. 'You know that every girl on the estate, whether she's a groom or an *au pair*, is pure dirt in the gimlet eyes of the Cruikshank lassies.'

Nanny left Beirut before her gimlet eyes and the lady herself told her that Olive was pregnant again. Olive had had a few miscarriages and two children who'd died in infancy, but she and Ranald still hoped for another boy so that Cameron need not bear alone the burden of family tradition.

*

Soon after Nanny Cruikshank left, Sir Ranald took his wife and son to a large seaside hotel several miles from Tripoli. Their Egyptian *au pair*, Faerida, came with them to keep Cameron company while his mother was resting and his father was away to Beirut for diplomatic meetings. Faerida, a rather overblown sixteen, quickly became acquainted with a soldier at the barracks outside the village, so she and Cameron came to an understanding: as long as Cameron did not tell his parents, Faerida would leave the boy alone to do what he liked.

Cameron spent a lot of time exploring the ruins of the Saracen's castle on the cliff a mile from the hotel. And it was on the castle battlements that he first encountered Mr Sulieman Hikmet.

Cameron had witnessed Mr Hikmet's arrival at the hotel. It had impressed him. It was an arrival embellished by much scurrying of Arab page-boys carrying Mr Hikmet's pile of expensive luggage while Mr Hikmet stood in the centre of the foyer waving a long thin gold-topped cane, shouting instructions and once, to Cameron's horror, striking one of the pages on the bottom with his cane.

Cameron remembered this when he came face to face with Mr Hikmet at the top of the castle that afternoon. Mr Hikmet still carried his cane, though it was so slender and delicate it could not have been any help to him in his climb to the battlements. He was a large stout man who seemed old to Cameron. The boy had heard his father telling his mother: 'The fellow's a bit of a git by the look of him, millionaire or no millionaire. He's over-weight and over-oily. He waddles like a dirty old duck, m'dear. About my own age, I'd think.'

Cameron knew his father was forty. He could not believe that Mr Hikmet with his large pockmarked nose, thick lips and skull of close-cropped grey hair was anywhere near as young as his jolly, effervescent good-looking and boyish Dad, always game for a lark.

'The little English boy!' Mr Hikmet greeted Cameron on that first afternoon. 'I see you in hotel. *Bon jour*, English boy. How are you?'

'*Je suis* smashing, *monsieur*,' Cameron said. 'And please, monsieur, I am not English. I am Scottish.'

'English! Scottish! What does it matter, eh? You go school in England?'

Cameron said: '*Oui, monsieur*.'

'You go Rugby?'

Cameron said nothing. He was watching the sweat glisten on the Turk's wobbling jowls, and the beads of moisture sliding out of the huge pores of his bulbous nose.

'Dr Arnold! Cold baths! Beatings!' The Turk sniggered. Cameron turned his head and looked down at the waves dashing against the rocks far below.

The Turk placed a plump hand on the boy's head and pressed it down. Cameron's scalp crawled with distaste. 'Pretty English boy,' Mr Hikmet lisped. 'Your master beat you?'

'Scottish,' Cameron said. 'And he doesn't.'

Mr Hikmet giggled. He flicked Cameron's bottom with his cane, then he let it slide caressingly down the boy's thighs. Cameron shivered as the cold wood touched his bare skin.

'Don't do that,' he said.

The fat Turk giggled. 'Say please!'

Cameron glared at him. 'Excuse me,' he said, moving past the man, 'My parents are waiting for me.'

And he ran down the worn old slabs of stair and did not

slacken his pace until he was well beyond the castle's archway.

*

That evening when Cameron and his parents and Faerida were waiting for the elevator to take them to the restaurant on the hotel roof, Mr Hikmet joined them. 'Aha, my little English friend!' he said, putting his hand on Cameron's shoulder. 'You must introduce me to Mama and Papa. And this beautiful young lady. She is your sister?'

He was carrying his cane. In the crowded elevator he stood behind Cameron and pushed its gold tip into the base of the boy's spine, grinding it like a chemist grinding a pestle in a mortar. When Cameron jerked forward, Mr Hikmet pulled him back and held the boy firmly against him.

'I can't stand that man,' Olive Locherbie said when they were seated at their own table, having resisted Mr Hikmet's attempts to stay with them.

'Don't be so ridiculously Auld Kirk, Ollie,' Sir Ranald said, 'You're as bad as Nanny. There's nothing wrong with the fellow, except he's too fat and laughs too much. And why does he carry that grotty cane? All right if he was on a horse, but no bloody good for walking. Got no body in it. What the fellow needs is a stick as stout as himself. But why bring it to the dining room? He's not lame.'

'He's a *poseur*,' Olive said. 'He keeps wanting to draw attention to himself. There's something slimy about him that I can't bear. He gives me the grue. Don't you have anything to do with him, Cameron. I heard his inviting you to go for a walk with him tomorrow. Well, don't.'

'I won't, Mummy. I told him I couldn't.'

'Cassandra of the League for Presbyterian Purity!' Ranald said, laughing. 'Honestly, dear, you take the bloody biscuit. Stop behaving like Jenny Geddes throwing her stool at the poor old Archbishop. You and Nan! What a mercy she's not here. She'd have been after poor old Hikmet with bell, book and candle.'

'I wouldn't blame her,' Olive said. 'There's something evil … something dreadfully uncanny about the man … '

*

Cameron dodged Mr Hikmet successfully for several days. The only times he allowed the Turk to speak to him were when he was in the foyer or with his parents or Faerida. It was difficult, though, to avoid him outside the hotel, for Mr Hikmet was always walking on the mile of beach between the hotel and the castle. So, unless he went on the terrace, which usually was crowded with other visitors, Cameron stayed in the foyer close to Leo, the tall smiling young Nigerian at the reception desk. There were no children of Cameron's age in the hotel, but he and Leo were attracted to each other, and Cameron felt safe when he was within his big black friend's orbit. Leo was an archeological student at the French university in Beirut, and he had taken this hotel job for the summer.

It was Leo who took Cameron in the first place to the Saracen's castle on the cliff. The castle had been a stronghold in the days of the Crusades, and many of its old battlements and defences still remained. Leo told Cameron a great deal about the original layout and the customs of the Moslems who had lived there, and the boy was so fascinated by the pinkish-beige ruins with their subterranean passages and strange nooks that he visited them alone several times without anything out of the ordinary happening. The ruins were always deserted except for sea birds and lizards and small scurrying animals. But after Mr Hikmet's arrival, although still drawn towards the castle, Cameron did not dare approach it in case he met the Turkish millionaire either on the beach or on the rough track leading past the garrison and through the sand dunes. If he met Mr Hikmet among the high lonely sand dunes it would be almost impossible to escape from him.

Three days after the fat Turk's arrival, Leo managed to get some free time, and he again took Cameron to the castle. They explored the dungeons beneath the ruins: parts of which Cameron had been afraid to enter when alone. Some of the dungeons were still in much the same condition as they had been in centuries ago, but the walls of others had collapsed, leaving only great black holes that reeked of rotten vegetation, from the depth of which the bright eyes of rodents appeared like miniature searchlights.

Cameron kept close to Leo as they scrambled over the piles

of fallen stones and wormed their way from one dark cavern to the next. Their torch-beams picked out bits of rusty iron chains still hanging from the walls, and in one dark corner the remains of a great bench studded with barbaric iron brackets and spikes. 'I certainly don't take to the place, Cameron boy,' Leo said. 'It's got a voodoo. There's something real evil about it. It doesn't bear to think about what men did to other men in these dark holes. C'mon, let's get out of here quick-quick before we start meeting spooks.'

Cameron shivered and clung to Leo's warm comforting waist. They climbed to the top of the battlements to get welcome sea-fresh air. Leaning against a broken turret, they watched Mr Hikmet walking on the beach far below. He was wearing a dark reddish suit, and he resembled a large undecided crab as he kept pausing uncertainly and poking in the sand with his thin stick. Leo grinned at Cameron, then he bent over the parapet and spat in Mr Hikmet's direction. He made some esoteric signs with his hands. 'My people's way of warding off evil spirits, Cameron boy,' he said. 'But I wouldn't advise you to copy it. If you ever see anything bad, boy, you run away from it. Quick-quick. You listen to Leo and do that. Quick-quick.'

*

Next day, emboldened by his visit with Leo, Cameron went alone again to the castle. And it was then he encountered both Mr Sulieman Hikmet and the scarlet-haired boy who came out of thin air.

He ran as fast as he could to the hotel. He spoke to Leo for a few minutes but said nothing about Mr Hikmet and the strange boy. He knew his mother was resting, and he guessed his father would be writing letters or on the telephone to Beirut; so he went to his room and started to read C.S. Lewis's *The Horse and His Boy*, which Leo had given to him. But he could not concentrate. Even though he realised there was a similarity between his own detestation of Mr Hikmet and the boy Shasta's fear of becoming the slave of the Tarkaan lord who owned the talking horse Bree, he could not give the story his full attention for wondering about the boy with the scarlet hair. Where had he come from? Had he been hiding somewhere? Cameron had been in the castle for an hour before Mr Hikmet arrived. He had been alone in the ruins. Where had the boy been hiding? How had Cameron not seen him approaching the castle's gateway, which he had had under observation all the time? Had the boy Simon really come out of thin air as he had appeared to do? Was he one of the spooks in the dungeons that Leo had spoken about?

That evening, after dinner, Leo came to the Locherbies' sitting room to play cards with Cameron and Faerida. He told them with amusement that Mr Hikmet's manservant had been worried all afternoon because the millionaire had not returned from his after-lunch walk, and there had been a great commotion a short time ago when the Turk had arrived with his garments in a filthy state, his feet and legs wet, and behaving in a hysterical fashion.

'He says that you shut him in a dark hole in the old Saracen castle, Cameron, and then ran away and left him to die,' Leo said.

'*Quel menteur!*' Faerida cried. 'I was wis Cameron all day and we never see one tiny speck of that horrid Turkish man.'

'Of course, he's a liar,' Leo said, and he winked at Faerida; he knew she had spent most of the afternoon with her boy friend at the garrison. 'He says Cameron pushed him into the old dungeon and then rolled a great boulder in front of it so he couldn't get out for hours.'

'I never heard such bloody nonsense,' Sir Ranald said, looking up from the diplomatic papers he was supposed to be reading. 'I'm not denying that Sunshine here is a pretty good strong boy for his age, but I'm darned if I can see him doing this to a man of that fat git's weight. I'll have a word with the fellow.'

'What a shit the man is,' Lady Locherbie said. 'But what else can you expect from a man with his background? They say he was a rag and bone man before he became a millionaire.'

'The fellow's just a jumped-up git,' Ranald said. 'He's got no breeding. He'll be more hysterical by the time I'm through with him.'

'Y'know, there's something terribly old, something terribly evil about him.' Olive Locherbie shivered. 'I can't bear the sight of him. Those oily chops ... '

'Mr Hikmet has lost his stick,' Leo said, shuffling the cards.

'No harm,' Sir Ranald said. 'Grotty stupid thing – like the grotty stupid clot himself. I say!' He grinned at them all. 'Do excuse me for using such an outdated jargon word. I don't particularly care for it, but it seems to suit the fellow.'

'He is a super clot, sir,' Leo said.

'Super clot or not, we should all steer clear of him,' Olive Locherbie said. 'And you, Cameron, steer clear of that old ruin as well. It bodes no good.'

*

Despite his mother's warning, Cameron set off early next morning for the Saracen's castle. Leo had told him that Mr Hikmet was still in bed, suffering from shock, and was likely to remain there for a time.

There was something so menacing about the ruins high above the great piercing spray-splashed rocks that Cameron was tempted to stay on the sandy beach, heed his mother's warning, call it a day and retrace his steps. But he was determined to find the scarlet haired boy, Simon, so he climbed towards the archway leading into the ruins, every nerve alert.

There was no sign of a living soul anywhere. Cameron went up the worn stone steps to his favourite seat in the embrasure of one of the towers. At the top of the steps was Mr Hikmet's gold-topped cane. Cameron kicked it aside and went to the embrasure. He sat down with his back to the sea, so that he could see anyone approach the gateway from all sides. He had been sitting for ten minutes when a voice said:

'So you have come back, *mon cher*, to release my ghost from bondage?'

The Christian boy called Simon stood beside him.

'I willed you to come back,' Simon said. 'I knew you'd come because of the ties of blood. For only someone of my own blood can free me from bondage.'

Cameron said: 'Are you truly a ghost?'

'I am truly a ghost.' Simon sat beside him and put a hand on Cameron's knee. Although it was cold, it felt like any other boy's hand, and the shoulder pressing against Cameron's was solid enough.

'I am one of your ancestors,' Simon said. 'In truth, I am not one of your forebears, for I died in the year 1213 when I was eleven years old. But my father was Sir Uchtred de Locherbie, and I presume you are descended from the child my lady mother was carrying when I set off on the Crusade.'

'There are several Uchtreds in our family tree,' Cameron said.

'And many Simons?'

'The eldest son is always christened Simon,' Cameron said. 'It has been a custom for hundreds of years, though he had several other names attached and often is called by one of these. I was christened Simon Alexander Uchtred Cameron, and my father is Simon Ranald Uchtred.'

'My ghost may be allowed to return to Scotland if you will help me,' Simon said. 'I have longed for over seven hundred years to leave this Moslem castle and go home.'

'But how can I help you?' Cameron said.

'By killing the Emir Sulieman.'

Cameron stared at the boy who might have been his twin: examining his features he saw every time he looked in a mirror. Simon smiled and said: 'I was one of the boys who went on the Children's Crusade, and I was sold into slavery. Can you think what that meant? Can you imagine how I felt to be handled and caressed and whipped, depending on the mood of a fat sweaty old Moslem emir? Our family is of Norman blood, and you know how proud we are.'

Simon had a thin gold chain round his neck. A huge gold Islamic crescent dangled from it. Seeing the movement of Cameron's eyes, the ghost-boy touched it and said: 'The Saracens hung these on their horses' bridles and on their foreheads. They also hung them on their slaves. They are said to ward off the evil eye.'

'And did it?' Cameron said.

Simon laughed. '*Au contraire, mon cher*, I think it encouraged it. My master's eye was more evil than Satan's.'

'Why did you go on the Children's Crusade?'

'Because my father told me to join and give honour to our house.' Simon shaded his eyes and looked along the beach. 'The Emir is coming,' he said. 'There is just time to tell you about my short life before he arrives – to meet retribution at your hands.'

'But I can't kill Mr Hikmet,' Cameron said. 'He hasn't really done me any harm. My mother says he's evil, and I think he is, but he hasn't actually *done* anything to me.'

'He has sullied the honour of our house,' Simon said. 'He must perish. Only when he perishes – and your Mr Hikmet *is* the Emir Sulieman in human guise – will my spirit be free to go home.'

*

'Though where my home is I cannot truly say,' Simon said. 'Is it Scotland? Or is it France? I was born at Ardavalloch, but I spent more than half my eleven years in France. My father was a friend of our king, William the Lion, and I was brought up with the king's son Alexander. He was four years my elder and I was supposed to be his page. I had a serf of my own, Donald, a boy from the north, my own age. When Alexander adopted too princely a manner, Donald and I united against him. The only time we were not able to overpower him was when he refused to go on the Children's Crusade. We were in France then, on one of the great estates King William had inherited from his mother. The king wished Prince Alexander to become a good Frank, so he put my sire, who was more a Frank than a Scot, in charge of the Prince's household, to act *in loco parentis* when he himself was in Scotland. In the year 1212 we went to the Abbey of Saint-Denis to attend the French court. And there, alas, Alexander and Donald and I listened to the ravings of Stephen, a shepherd boy, who said he had a letter from the Lord Jesus Christ telling him to preach a new Crusade. Stephen was an unlearned peasant, but he had imagination and such a gift of oratory that thousands of children – girls as well as boys – flocked around him and swore they'd follow him to the Holy Land. One of Stephen's prophecies was that the Mediterranean would open wide – as the Red Sea had opened to the Israelites – and he and all his followers would be able to march on dry ground all the way to Outremer.'

'Outremer?' Cameron said. 'I thought you said the crusade was going to the Holy Land?'

'Outremer is what this part of the world was called then,' Simon said. 'The Holy Land is only a small part of Outremer. My sire also listened to some of Stephen's ravings. Sir Uchtred thought it fitting that Prince Alexander should join the crusade and lead it instead of the half-daft peasant boy. He invited Alexander to volunteer, but His Highness wouldn't. His Highness was now fifteen and looked on himself as a full-fledged knight. Sir Uchtred was so angry at his pupil's disobedience that forthwith he ordered me and Donald to join the crusade, hoping Prince Alexander would be ashamed and follow our example. But Alexander did not, so, urged on by my sire, Donald and I rode off alone to Vendôme and joined the thousands of children gathered around Stephen. It was my sire's wish that, since Alexander would not lead the crusade, I should take his place. If he had not pictured me leading the young crusaders to glory, I believe Sir Uchtred would not have sent his only son on such a mission. But Stephen would not listen to my argument that I was by birth and breeding a rightful leader; he said rudely he was God's appointed, and as he was a year my senior and very strong I had perforce to submit. We even had to submit to our ponies being taken from us and sold to buy food for our fellow pilgrims. And so it was in no great state of grace or happiness that we arrived in the port of Marseilles. By this time many of our young fellow crusaders had died or turned homewards. Donald argued that our journey seemed futile and we should return to Varenne, but I did not wish to stir up my father's ire. I still do not know whether, like Stephen, we expected the waters of the Mediterranean to open wide and display a dry path, but if we did we were deceived. The Mediterranean remained deep and dark and blue in front of us. And then two kind-hearted merchants, Hugh and William, said they would give us seven ships and would take us free of charge in them to the Holy Birthplace. These kind gentlemen wanted no recompense. All they required was that we should recite their names in our prayers when eventually we reached Jerusalem.'

'And did you?' Cameron said.

'You are ignorant, aren't you?' Simon said. 'I would have hoped for a Locherbie to show more historical knowledge than – shall we say – a peasant like Stephen in his stinking shepherd's clothes.'

'I'm sorry,' Cameron said.

'You should be, but I forgive you,' Simon looked down into the ruins of the bailey. 'The Emir approaches. It will still, however, be a few minutes before he reaches this place of destiny.'

He continued: 'We had been at sea only a few days when our ships were seized by pirates in the pay of William and Hugh. We were all taken to the North African coast and sold. Donald and I were sold in the slave market at Alexandria. I don't know what happened to Donald after that. I was bought by fat Emir Sulieman and brought to this castle. Sulieman was – he still is – a wicked man, and I will not tell you how badly he treated me. He used to take me to his bed and make me do disgusting things. When I wouldn't, he whipped me and had me chained in a dungeon. Sometimes he was slobbering over me with lust; at other times he was like a glacier in his indifference to mercy. Often he threatened to sell me to the Bedouins. I knew that when I grew bigger and he lost interest in me he would send me to the galleys. The Emir tried to make me become a Moslem, but I refused. All his slaves and soldiers hated me because I was a Christian. The only one who was kind was Amar, a big Numidian eunuch. He often brought me sweetmeats when I was in the dungeon, and he would take me in his arms and comfort me for hours and make the darkness less frightening and keep the rats away. I loved Amar. One night Amar told me that he and I would escape together and flee far from the Emir, and he promised to free me from the chains next day.'

Cameron said: 'And did he?'

The ghost-boy sighed: 'No. Next morning the Emir himself

came and had the chains taken off. Then he drove me in front of him with his stick into the castle's bailey. And what I saw there made me scream. Amar, my big warm-hearted Amar, was strung up on a gibbet. He was not dead, and some Saracen soldiers were doing unspeakable things to his naked body. I knew I could do nothing to help him, so I ran towards the gateway. The Emir ran after me shouting: 'Wait, Christian boy, and watch your friend die slowly, slowly!' Soldiers headed me off, and I ran up the stairs to the battlements. The Emir followed close, striking me with his stick. I leapt on that battlement there and ran along the top, and then ... The Emir kept poking me with his stick, and I slipped and fell on to the rocks below.'

*

'Good morning, English boy,' Mr Hikmet said.

Cameron rose from his seat in the embrasure and watched the fat Turk climb wheezily up the stone stairs. He put out his hand to clasp Simon's but felt only empty air. Yet he knew Simon was still there, so putting on a bold face he walked towards the Turk.

Mr Hikmet leered and said: 'I have come to punish you, English boy, for what happen yesterday. You are a wicked boy.'

'I am a Scottish boy,' Cameron said. 'How often must I tell you this? Please let me pass.'

'No, no! *Un moment*!' Mr Hikmet's foot kicked his stick. His eyes glistened and he pounced, a plump bird of prey. 'So you have the instrument of punishment in readiness! Thank you, thank you, Scottish boy, it will give me great pleasure.' He put out his hand to hold Cameron's arm. 'You kiss my stick, Scottish boy, and you say: "I am sorry, master. I kneel before you, master." '

'Fuck off,' Cameron said.

And he pushed past the Turk, giving his protruding stomach a violent jab with his elbow. The Turk tried to grab Cameron's shoulder but the jab had upset his balance and he fell against the boy instead. Cameron was sent spinning. The Turk raised his stick and screamed.

'Run, Cameron,' Simon said, appearing out of the air.

The Turk stared at the ghost-boy with amazement. 'Two boys! Twins!' he cried. 'You play no more tricks on me. I beat you both. And I complain to Papa who will beat you again.'

It was impossible for Cameron to get near the steps, so he ran towards the battlements. Simon followed, running backwards before Mr Hikmet, who kept yelling and waving his stick. Cameron leaped on top of the thick stone parapet and started to walk to the ruined tower growing out of it; he could climb the wall at the end of the parapet and so elude Mr Hikmet, that stout crab incapable of tackling anything so high. But before he could reach the wall, he discovered that Mr Hikmet had managed to scramble on top of the parapet and was close behind him.

'Cameron, don't go any further,' Simon called. 'Wait.'

And he danced on the parapet between Cameron and the Turk. Mr Hikmet came forward cautiously and poked his stick at Simon. 'Aha! I got both boys now! You not escape from Sulieman the Magnificent!'

He pushed his stick at Simon and it went through the ghost and touched Cameron on the chest.

'Seize it!' Simon shouted.

Cameron grabbed the thin end and tried to push it away, but it was so supple that it bent towards the empty air above the sea, and it brought Mr Hikmet almost on top of him. Simon had dissolved. In a frenzy of fear, Cameron flung out the arm grasping the stick. The movement upset Mr Hikmet's balance again. He staggered unsteadily, gave a great scream and fell over the parapet.

It was several seconds before Cameron could stop trembling. He had his hands clapped over his ears to drown the screams. He opened his eyes. There was no sign of Simon. Cameron cautiously climbed off the parapet, then he leaned over and looked down. Mr Hikmet lay on the rocks below, white waves already splashing over his insignificant body. Cameron wiped the cold sweat off his face, and he looked again for Simon. There was still no sign, but from high above the nearest tower his voice called:

'*Bien merci, mon frère.*'

The tall black figure of Leo was leaning against the tower wall. Cameron started to cry with relief as he ran towards him. Leo clasped the boy in his arms.

'I saw it all,' he said. 'It was his own fault. He chased you onto the parapet. I will tell everybody what a wicked man he was, and how he deserved to die.'

Cameron snuggled into the warmth of Leo's big body, and they walked towards the steps. Suddenly there was the sound of wings flapping. They looked up at a great sea bird with a scarlet crest poised on top of the tallest tower. It hovered for a moment, then they watched it circle slowly over them, the sun shining on its crest, before it flew off towards the north-west.

IV

All In The Mind

Chris Simons

I have often felt there must be rational explanations for most so-called supernatural experiences. For example, one of my former friends used to have frequent contacts with the spirit world, usually after having a few drinks. Without exception these happenings seemed to be preceded by tell-tale clues – acute depression, thunder and lightning, pins and needles – anything to set the scene. But, in my case, there was nothing to warn me of what was about to happen.

It had been one of those blue and gold September days, warm and balmy with a beautiful sunset. I had spent the afternoon and evening with friends who lived in a secluded cottage on the North coast of Cornwall, on that narrow spit of land approaching Land's End. Before dinner we had walked down to a nearby cove where the sea washed seaweed-strewn, grey rocks and where seals sometimes ventured on a calm day.

Naturally we had a glass of wine or two with our meal, but that was hours before I left. I found the conversation more intoxicating than the wine, as we discussed everything including politics, sex and religion, enjoying our arguments as only good friends can do. The atmosphere had been light-hearted, and we had spent most of the evening playing cards. Any bridge enthusiast would have been badly shaken by the way in which we abused that serious game, but the cheating was part of our enjoyment and we were happy novices rather than enthusiasts.

Time had passed too swiftly, as it invariably does in the

company of friends, and it was after midnight when I finally left the cottage. The night was still, silent except for the faint rustling of leaves and the murmur of a nearby stream. The velvet black sky sparkled with stars, although there was no moon, and a solitary glow worm lit my path from a low bush. I climbed into the car, and set off home in a pleasantly contented state of mind.

As I guided my vehicle down the bumpy lane from the cottage, I smiled at a familiar sight. A shaggy grey shape ambled slowly in front of me – an old badger I had often followed before. He always seemed unconcerned by the lights of the car or the noise of the engine, and never moved from the centre of the lane until he reached a certain gap in the hedgerow. Sometimes, on the same journey, I glimpsed other wild creatures – foxes and rabbits, and once a weasel streaked across the lane in front of me. It was all part of the attraction of that small corner of Cornwall.

I had just turned off the coast road, which runs from Zennor into St Ives, when the car began to splutter and jolt. Easing my foot off the accelerator, I changed gear, but the car continued to jerk spasmodically until finally the engine cut out. Almost immediately I realised what I had done. The choke was still out and I had flooded the engine with petrol. This was not the first time I had made this mistake, so I knew what to do. If I waited for a few moments and then tried to start the car again it would probably be all right. I switched off the lights and leaned back to wait.

The lane through the village of Towednack is narrow and twisting. All around, the hills are strewn with lonely granite boulders – the remnants, some say, of long-forgotten battles between ancient Cornish giants. This area is a part of primaeval West Penwith, where the undulating hills and valleys are threaded with old tin-mine workings, proclaimed here and there by the skeletal remains of engine houses.

Towednack village boasts a few trees and a scattering of farms and cottages, dominated by the unusually squat tower of an old granite church. It was a place through which I had passed frequently until that night.

As I sat in the car, waiting to try the ignition again, I

suddenly noticed a change in the night. The thousands of stars had disappeared completely, and long tentacles of mist were weaving across the road, wrapping themselves around my car. There was an unusual luminousness about the hedgerows, and I began to shiver. The night had a strange new chill. I pulled the starter and my old car spluttered reluctantly back to life. Turning the headlights on full, I began to move forward very slowly. The lights bounced back at me, making little impression on the gathering mist.

Driving needed all my concentration in such circumstances, but my mind was distracted. Gone was all my earlier contentment, replaced by prickling sensations of fear. I am not superstitious, but I certainly could not explain the clammy coldness which was creeping through my body or the unearthly terror which was slowly taking control of me. My knuckles were white where I clutched the steering wheel, as though it were the only thing that might save me from whatever threatened. My teeth were clenched so tightly that my jaw hurt. Why? I did not know why and could not rationalise my reactions. I just had a feeling – a strange unexplainable feeling.

Then I saw her. At least, I felt her presence first; knew there was someone or something in the car with me. That was a terrible sensation: I was deprived of my protection – the car had been my shell, shielding me or so I thought. A long, long time seemed to pass before I could turn my head away from the road ahead to look at whatever was sitting beside me.

In the darkness, the livid whiteness of her face startled me. It was impossible to tell where her flesh ended and the white material of her clothing began. The only relief from this whiteness was a slash of purple for a mouth and jet brows above the largest eyes I have ever seen. I remember her hair was straight and black, hanging loose down to her waist, but the eyes were really remarkable. Their baleful regard was hypnotic and would not allow me to tear my gaze away. I could not read any expression in those deep, dark orbs, but I could feel their intensity. Those eyes did not like me, but they were disguised by the darkness around us – unlike the emotion which emanated from the woman as a whole. Pure hatred, it was; she hated me intensely.

Even then I remember questioning her emotion. Who *was* she? *Why* did she hate me? Had I done something to cause such intense emotion to be directed at me? I searched my memory for some clue, but could not find anything. All human beings do some things which they later regret, and I am only human. But I have never deliberately hurt another person or done anything that might justify such hatred.

As her eyes continued to draw mine, I wondered again who she was and why she had come to *me*. Could it all be a mistake? Deep inside I knew it was no mistake. All the malevolence was directed at me personally. Perhaps it was a warning about something I might do, rather than something I had done. I could not accept that this hatred was without reason, or that the woman's appearance in *my* car was pure chance. With a supreme effort, I tore myself away from those hypnotic eyes and stared fixedly at the road ahead.

I drove on; I was incapable of doing anything else. My foot sank down on the accelerator and I flew along the lane by instinct, hardly able to see the road for the swirling mist. Perhaps, I thought that by speeding I could leave this hostile presence behind. But she stayed with me, permeating the atmosphere with her hatred.

Again, I questioned my experience, my sensations. Perhaps she was just a jealous woman – someone who had been rejected by my lover. That was an explanation at least – even if it did not fully explain how she happened to be sitting beside me now. Had I fallen asleep when the car stopped? She might have climbed in beside me then. It was no use. Even while thinking of all those possibilities, I knew she was not real – at least not physically.

My car was almost flying along the lane, but the woman was still there beside me. She stayed with me until the moment when I turned into the road from St Ives to Penzance, close to the next village of Nancledra. At that moment, the mist disappeared and I could see the stars again. Then I knew she had gone away.

Slowly and carefully now, I continued my journey. My clothes were drenched with perspiration and yet I was shivering. I turned the heater on to full, but it did not help at all. Hate must be the most powerful of the emotions, and I knew I should never forget the intensity of that woman's hatred. I realised she had been a spectre and I realised something else too: something which frightened me even more than the experience itself. Quite suddenly and inexplicably, I knew she was the spectre of a living person, and of someone I knew well. The really terrible thing was that I did not know the identity of that person.

You may say I have an over-active imagination. Perhaps, you think, it was due to nervousness. After all, breaking down in a lonely country lane in the early hours of the morning is not a pleasant experience. But, if you had felt that hatred or seen those dark, unfathomable eyes, you would believe me.

Three weeks later, I had my first nervous breakdown. Nothing helped. My doctor gave me tranquillisers and sleeping tablets. I tried whisky. Whatever I did, she was still there, staring at me and accusing me of some unspeakable crime. Again and again, I felt her hatred surrounding me, smothering me.

My friends were kind and sympathetic at first. They listened to me with patience. But then I began to wonder which of *them* was the woman. I could not trust them any longer. I knew she was there somewhere, hiding behind the face of a friend. Suspicion poisoned my friendships, as I searched each pair of eyes for that malevolence I had felt one misty night. I drove them away one by one.

Eventually, even my lover turned his back on me. I had become neurotic with fear: so convinced that spectral woman resented our relationship that I destroyed it myself. As I drove him away, I was fully aware of what I was doing, but could no longer help myself. Only when he had gone did I realise she had not cared about our relationship, because she still continued to haunt me.

Time has passed since that first breakdown, and my psychiatrist has tried everything to rationalise the experience of an early September morning. Nothing works and I have never driven along that country lane since. Perhaps one day I shall do so – if only to confront my spectre again. Perhaps, by then, I shall know which of my acquaintances hates me so intensely. But maybe, as my psychiatrist suggests, I shall only meet myself in that dark and misty lane.

V

The Labyrinth

R. Chetwynd-Hayes

They were lost. Rosemary knew it and said so in forceful language. Brian was also well aware of their predicament but was unwilling to admit it.

'One cannot be lost in England,' he stated. 'We're bound to strike a main road if we walk in a straight line.'

'But suppose we wander in a circle?' Rosemary asked, looking fearfully round at the Dartmoor landscape, 'and finish up in a bog?'

'If we use our eyes there's no reason why bogs should bother us. Come on and stop moaning.'

'We should never have left that truck,' Rosemary insisted. 'Suppose we get caught out here when night falls?'

'Don't be daft,' he snapped, 'it's only mid-day. We'll be in Princetown long before nightfall.'

'You hope.' She refused to be convinced. 'I'm hungry.'

'So am I.' They were walking up a steep incline. 'But I don't keep on about it.'

'I'm not keeping on. I'm hungry and I said so. Do you think we'll find a main road soon?'

'Over the next rise,' he promised. 'There's always a main road over the next rise.'

But he was wrong. When they crested the next rise and looked down, there was only a narrow track which terminated at a tumbledown gate set in a low stone wall. Beyond, like an island girdled by a yellow lake, was a lawn-besieged house. It was built of grey stone and seemed to have been thrown up by the moors; a great, crouching monster that glared out across the countryside with multiple glass eyes. It had a strange look. The chimney stacks might have been jagged splinters of rock that had acquired a rough cylindrical shape after centuries of wind and rain. But the really odd aspect was that the sun appeared to ignore the house. It had baked the lawn to a pale yellow, cracked the paint on an adjacent summerhouse, but in some inexplicable way, it seemed to disavow the existence of the great, towering mass.

'Tea!' exclaimed Rosemary.

'What?'

'Tea.' She pointed. 'The old lady, she's drinking tea.'

Sure enough, seated by a small table that nestled in the shade of a vast multi-coloured umbrella was a little white-haired old lady taking tea. Brian frowned, for he could not understand why he had not seen her, or at least the umbrella, before, but there she was, a tiny figure in a white dress and a floppy hat, sipping tea and munching sandwiches. He moistened dry lips.

'Do you suppose,' he asked, 'we dare intrude?'

'Watch me,' Rosemary started running down the slope towards the gate. 'I'd intrude on Dracula himself if he had a decent cup of tea handy.'

Their feet moved on to a gravel path and it seemed whatever breeze stirred the sun-warm heather out on the moors did not dare intrude here. There was a strange stillness, a complete absence of sound, save for the crunch of feet on gravel, and this too ceased when they walked on to the parched lawn.

The old lady looked up and a slow smile gradually lit up a benign, wizened little face, while her tiny hands fluttered over the table, setting out two cups and saucers, then felt the teapot as though to make sure the contents were still hot.

'You poor children.' Her voice had that harsh, slightly cracked quality peculiar to some cultured ladies of an advanced age, but the utterance was clear, every word pronounced with precision. 'You look so hot and tired.'

'We're lost,' Rosemary announced cheerfully. 'We've wandered for miles.'

'I must apologise for intruding,' Brian began, but the old

lady waved a teaspoon at him as though to stress the impossibility of intrusion.

'My dear young man – please. You are most welcome. I cannot recall when I last entertained a visitor, although I have always hoped someone might pass this way again. The right kind of someone, of course.'

She appeared to shiver momentarily, or perhaps tremble, for her hands and shoulders shook slightly, then an expression of polite distress puckered her forehead.

'But how thoughtless I am. You are tired having wandered so many miles and there are no chairs.'

She turned her head and called out in a high-pitched, quivering voice. 'Carlo! Carlo!'

A tall, lean man came out of the house and moved slowly towards them. He was dressed in a black satin tunic and matching trouers and, due possibly to some deformity, appeared to bound over the lawn, rather than walk. Brian thought of a wolf, or a large dog that has spotted intruders. He stopped a few feet from the old lady and stood waiting, his slate-coloured eyes watching Rosemary with a strange intensity.

'Carlo, you will fetch chairs,' the old lady ordered, 'then some more hot water.'

Carlo made a guttural sound and departed in the direction of the summerhouse, leaping forward in a kind of loping run. He returned almost immediately carrying two little slatted chairs and presently Brian and Rosemary were seated under the vast umbrella, drinking tea from delicate china cups and listening to the harsh, cultivated voice.

'I must have lived alone here for such a long time. Gracious me, if I were to tell you how long, you would smile. Time is such an inexhaustible commodity, so long as one can tap the fountainhead. The secret is to break it down into small change. An hour does not seem to be long until you remember it has three thousand, six hundred seconds. And a week! My word, did you ever realise you have six hundred and four thousand, eight hundred seconds to spend every seven days? It's an enormous treasure. Do have another strawberry jam sandwich, child.'

Rosemary accepted another triangular, pink-edged sandwich, then stared open-eyed at the house. At close quarters it looked even more grim than from a distance. There was the impression the walls had drawn their shadows above themselves like a ghostly cloak, and although the house stood stark and forbidding in broad daylight, it still seemed to be divorced from sunshine. Rosemary of course made the obvious statement.

'It must be very old.'

'It has lived,' the old lady said, 'for millions upon millions of seconds. It has drunk deep from the barrel of time.'

Rosemary giggled, then hastily assumed an extravagantly serious expression as Brian glared at her. He sipped his tea and said: 'This is really most kind of you. We were fagged out – and rather scared too. The moors seemed to go on and on and I thought we would have to spend the night out there.'

The old lady nodded, her gaze flickering from one young face to the other.

'It is not pleasant to be lost in a great, empty space. Doubtless, if you had not returned before nightfall, someone would have instigated a search for you.'

'Not on your nelly,' Rosemary stated with charming simplicity. 'No one knows where we are. We're sort of taking a roaming holiday.'

'How adventurous,' the old lady murmured, then called back over one shoulder. 'Carlo, the hot water, man. Do hurry.'

Carlo came bounding out of the house carrying a silver jug in one hand and a plate of sandwiches in the other. When he reached the table his mouth was open and he was breathing heavily. The old lady shot him an anxious glance.

'Poor old boy,' she consoled. 'Does the heat get you down, then? Eh? Does the heat make you puff and pant? Never mind, you can go and lie down somewhere in the shade.' She turned to her guests and smiled a most kindly, benign smile. 'Carlo has mixed blood and he finds the heat most trying. I keep telling him to practise more self-control, but he will insist on running about.' She sighed. 'I suppose it is his nature.'

Rosemary was staring intently at her lap and Brian saw an ominous shake of her shoulders, so he hurriedly exclaimed:

'You really live all alone in that vast house? It looks enormous.'

'Only a small portion, child.' She laughed softly, a little silvery sound. 'You see the windows on the ground floor which have curtains? That is my little domain. All the rest is closed up. Miles upon miles of empty corridors.'

Brian re-examined the house with renewed interest. Six lower windows looked more wholesome than the others; the frames had, in the not-too-distant past, been painted white and crisp white curtains gave them a lived-in look, but the panes still seemed reluctant to reflect the sunlight and he frowned before raising his eyes to the upper storeys.

Three rows of dirt-grimed glass: so many eyes from behind which life had long since departed, save possibly for rats and mice. Then he started and gripped his knees with hands that were not quite steady. On the topmost storey, at the window third from the left, a face suddenly emerged and pressed its nose flat against the glass. There was no way of telling if the face were young or old, or if it belonged to a man, woman or child. It was just a white blur equipped with a pair of blank eyes and a flattened nose.

'Madam … ' Brian began.

'My name,' the old lady said gently, 'is Mrs Brown.'

'Mrs Brown. There's a … '

'A nice homely name,' Mrs Brown went on. 'Do you not think so? I feel it goes with a blazing fire, a singing kettle and muffins for tea.'

'Madam – Mrs Brown. The window up there … '

'What window, child?' Mrs Brown was examining the interior of the teapot with some concern. 'There are so many windows.'

'The third from the left.' Brian was pointing at the face, which appeared to be opening and shutting its mouth. 'There is someone up there and they seem to be in trouble.'

'You are mistaken, my dear,' Mrs Brown shook her head. 'No one lives up there. And without life, there can be no face. That is logic.'

The face disappeared. It was not so much withdrawn as blotted out, as though the window had suddenly clouded over and now it was just another dead man's eye staring out over the sun-drenched moors.

'I could swear there was a face,' Brian insisted, and Mrs Brown smiled.

'A cloud reflection. It is so easy to see faces where none exist. A crack in the ceiling, a damp patch on the wall, a puddle in moonlight – all become faces when the brain is tired. Can I press you to another cup?'

'No, thank you.' Brian rose and nudged Rosemary to do the same. She obeyed with ill grace. 'If you would be so kind as to direct us to the nearest main road, we will be on our way.'

'I could not possibly do that.' Mrs Brown looked most distressed. 'We are really miles from anywhere and you poor children would get hopelessly lost. Really, I must insist you stay here for the night.'

'You are most kind and do not think us ungrateful,' Brian said, 'but there must be a village not too far away.'

'Oh, Brian,' Rosemary clutched his arm. 'I couldn't bear to wander about out there for hours. And suppose the sun sets ... ?'

'I've told you before we'll be home and dry long before then,' he snapped, and Mrs Brown rose, revealing herself as a figure of medium height, whose bowed shoulders made her shorter than she actually was. She shook a playful finger at the young man.

'How could you be so ungallant? Can you not see the poor girl is simply dropping from fatigue?' She took Rosemary's arm and began to propel her towards the house, still talking in her harsh, precise voice. 'These big strong men have no thought for us poor, frail women. Have they, my dear?'

'He's a brute.' Rosemary made a face at Brian over one shoulder. 'We wouldn't have got lost if he hadn't made us leave the main track.'

'It is the restless spirit that haunts the best of them,' Mrs Brown confided. 'They must wander into strange and forbidden places, then come crying home to us when they get hurt.'

They moved in through the open french windows, leaving the hot summer afternoon behind them, for a soft, clinging coolness leapt to embrace their bodies like a slightly damp sheet. Brian shivered, but Rosemary exclaimed: 'How sweet.'

She was referring to the room. It was full of furniture: chairs, table, sideboard, from which the sheen of newness had long since departed; the patterned carpet had faded, so had the wallpaper; a vase of dried flowers stood on the mantelpiece and from all around – an essential part of the coolness – came a sweet, just perceptible aroma. It was the scent of extreme old age which is timidly approaching death on faltering feet. For a moment, Brian had a mental picture of an open coffin with dying flowers. Then Mrs Brown spoke.

'There are two sweet little rooms situated at the rear. You will rest well in them.'

Carlo emerged from somewhere; he was standing by the open doorway, his slate-grey eyes watching Mrs Brown as she nodded gravely.

'Go with him, my dears. He will attend to your wants and presently, when you have rested, we will dine.'

They followed their strange guide along a gloom-painted passage and he silently opened two doors, motioned Rosemary into one, then, after staring blankly at Brian, pointed to the other.

'You've been with Mrs Brown a long time?' Brian asked in a loud voice, assuming the man was deaf. 'Must be rather lonely for you here.'

Carlo did not answer, only turned on his heel and went back along the passage with that strange, loping walk. Rosemary giggled.

'Honestly, did you ever see anything like it?'

'Only in a horror film,' Brian admitted. 'Say, do you suppose he's deaf and dumb?'

'Fairly obvious,' Rosemary shrugged. 'Let's have a look at our rooms.'

They were identical. Each held a four-poster bed, a Tudor-style chest of drawers and a bedside cupboard. The same faint odour prevailed here, but Rosemary did not seem to notice it.

'Do you suppose this place runs to a bath?' she asked, seating herself on Brian's bed.

Before he could answer, Carlo's lean form filled the doorway and he made a guttural sound while beckoning them to follow him. He led the way down the passage and at the very end opened a door and motioned them to enter the room beyond. It was empty save for a very ancient hip-bath and six leather buckets lined up against one wall.

They began to laugh, clinging to each other for support. Their silent guide watched them with an expressionless stare. Brian was the first to regain his powers of speech.

'Ask a silly question,' he gasped, 'and you'll get a ridiculous answer.'

*

'I rarely eat.'

Mrs Brown was sipping daintily from a glass of mineral water and watching the young people with lively interest as they each consumed a large steak and a generous helping of fresh salad.

'When you are my age,' she went on, 'one's fires need little fuel. A sip of water, an occasional nibble, the odd crumb.'

'But you must eat,' Rosemary looked at the old lady with some concern. 'I mean – you have to.'

'Child – ' Mrs Brown beckoned to Carlo who started to collect the empty plates, ' – food is not necessarily meat and vegetables. Passion will feed the soul and nourish the body. I recommend love as an *hors d'oeuvre,* hate as the *entrée* and fear as a chilly desert.'

Rosemary looked nervously at Brian, then took a long drink of water to hide her confusion. The young man decided to bring the conversation back to a more mundane plane.

'I am most interested in your house, Mrs Brown. It seems a shame that so little of it is used.'

'I did not say it was not used, dear,' Mrs Brown corrected gently. 'I said no one lived in the region that lies outside this apartment. There is, as I am sure you will agree, a difference.'

Carlo returned, carrying a dish of large, pink blancmange; this he deposited on the table after giving the girl and young man a long, expressionless stare.

'You must forgive Carlo,' Mrs Brown said while she carved the blancmange into thin slices. 'It is some time since we entertained guests and he is apt to stare at that which he is not allowed to touch.'

Brian nudged Rosemary, who was watching the blancmange carving with undisguised astonishment. 'Mrs Brown, you say the rest of the house is used, but not lived in. I'm sorry, but ... '

'Does anyone live in your stomach?' Mrs Brown asked quietly.

He laughed, but seeing no smile on the wrinkled face opposite quickly assumed a serious expression.

'No, of course not.'

'But it is used?' Mrs Brown persisted.

He nodded. 'Yes indeed. Quite a lot.'

'So with the house.' She handed Rosemary a plate that contained three thin slices of pink blancmange and the girl said 'Thank you' in a strangled voice. 'You see, the house does not require people to live in it, for the simple reason that it is, in itself, a living organism.'

Brian frowned as he accepted his plate of sliced blancmange.

'Why not?' The old lady appeared surprised that her word should be doubted. 'Do you begrudge a house life?'

They both shook their heads violently and Mrs Brown appeared satisfied with their apparent acquiescence.

'After all, in ordinary houses, what are passages? I will tell you. Intestines. Bowels, if you wish. And the boiler which pumps hot water throughout the body of the house? A heart – what else could it be? In the same way, that mass of pipes and cisterns that reside up in the loft, what are they if not a brain?'

'You have a point,' Brian agreed.

'Of course I have,' Mrs Brown deposited another slice of blancmange on Rosemary's plate. 'But of course I was referring to ordinary houses. This is not an ordinary house by any means. It really lives.'

'I would certainly like to meet the builder,' Brian said caustically. 'He must have been a remarkable chap.'

'Builder!' Mrs Brown chuckled. 'When did I mention a builder? My dear young man, the house was not built. It grew.'

*

'Nutty as a fruit cake.' Rosemary spoke with strong conviction while she sat on Brian's bed.

'True,' Brian nodded, 'but the idea is rather fascinating.'

'Oh, come off it. How can a house grow? And from what? A brick?'

'Wait a minute. In a way a house does grow. It is fathered by an architect and mothered by a builder.'

'That's all very well,' Rosemary complained, 'but that old sausage meant the damned thing grew like a tree. Frankly, she gives me the willies. You know something? I think she's laughing at us. I mean to say, all that business of carving blancmange into thin slices.'

'A house is an extension of a man's personality.' Brian was thinking out loud. 'In its early life it would be innocent, like a new-born baby, but after it had been lived in for a bit ... ' He paused, 'then the house would take on an atmosphere ... could even be haunted.'

'Oh, shut up.' Rosemary shivered. 'I'm expected to sleep here tonight. In any case, as I keep saying, the old thing maintains the house grew.'

'Even that makes a kind of mad logic.' He grinned, mocking what he assumed to be her pretended fear. 'We must reverse the process. The atmosphere came first, the house second.'

'I'm going to bed.' She got up and sauntered to the door. 'If you hear me scream during the night, come a-running.'

'Why bother to go?' Brian asked slyly. 'If you stay here, I won't have to run anywhere.'

'Ha, ha. Funny man. Not in this morgue.' She smiled impishly from the doorway. 'I'd be imagining all manner of things looking down at me from the ceiling.'

*

Brian lay in his four-poster bed and listened to the house preparing for sleep. Woodwork contracted as the temperature dropped; floorboards creaked, window frames made little rattling noises, somewhere a door closed. Sleep began to dull his senses and he became only half-aware of his surroundings; he was poised on the brink of oblivion. Then, as though a bomb had exploded, he was blasted back into full consciousness. A long drawn-out moan had shattered the silence and was coming at him from all directions. He sat up and looked round the room. So far as he could see by the light of the rising moon that filtered through his lace curtains, the room was empty. Suddenly, the groan was repeated. He sprang out of bed, lit his candle, and looked wildly around him. The sound was everywhere – in the walls with their faded pink-rose wallpaper, in the cracked ceiling, the threadbare carpet. He covered his ears with shaking hands, but still the mournful groan continued, invading his brain, seeping down into his very being, until it seemed the entire universe was crying out in anguish. Then, as abruptly as it began, it ceased. A heavy, unnatural silence descended on the house like a great, enveloping blanket. Brian hastily scrambled into his clothes.

'Enough is enough.' He spoke aloud. 'We're getting out – fast.'

Another sound came into being. It began a long way off. A slow, hesitant footstep, married to squeaking floorboards, a laborious picking up and putting down of naked feet, interspersed with a slow slithering which suggested the unseen walker was burdened with the tiredness of centuries. This time there was no doubt as to where the sound was coming from. It was up above. The soft, padding steps passed over the ceiling and once again the house groaned, but now it was a moan of ecstasy, a low cry of fulfilment. Brian opened the bedroom door and crept out into the corridor. The moaning cry and the slithering footsteps merged and became a nightmarish symphony, a two-toned serenade of horror. Then, again, all sound ceased and the silence was like a landmine that might explode at any moment. He found himself waiting for the moan, the slithering overhead footsteps to begin all over again – or perhaps something else, something that defied imagination.

He tapped on Rosemary's door, then turned the handle and entered, holding his candle high and calling her name.

'Rosemary, wake up. Rosemary, come on, we're getting out of here.'

The flickering candle-flame made great shadows leap across the walls and dance over the ceiling; it cut ragged channels through the darkness until, at last, his questing eye saw the bed. It was empty. The sheets and blankets were twisted up into loose ropes and a pillow lay upon the floor.

'Rosemary!'

He whispered her name and the house chuckled. A low, harsh, gurgling laugh, which made him run from the room, racing down the long corridor, until he lurched into the dining-room. An old-fashioned oil lamp stood on the table, illuminating the room with a pale orange light and revealing Mrs Brown, seated in an armchair, calmly darning a sock. She looked up as Brian entered and smiled like a mother whose small son has strayed from his warm bed in a winter's night.

'I would put the candle down, dear,' she said, 'otherwise you will spill grease all over the carpet.'

'Rosemary!' he shouted. 'Where is she?'

'There's really no need for you to shout. Despite my advanced years, I am not deaf.' She broke the wool, then turned the sock and examined her work with a certain pride. 'That's better. Carlo is so hard on his socks.' She looked up with a sly smile. 'It is only to be expected, of course. He has hard feet.'

'Where is she?' Brian set down the candle and moved closer to the old woman, who was now closing her work-basket. 'She's not in her room and there are signs of a struggle. What have you done with her?'

Mrs Brown shook her head sadly.

'Questions, questions. How hungry youth is for knowledge. You demand to know the truth and, should I gratify your desire, how distressed you would become. Ignorance is a gift freely offered by the gods and so often it is spurned by misguided mortals. Even I sometimes wish I knew less, but ... ' Her sigh was one of sad resignation. 'Time reveals all to those who live long enough. I should go back to bed, dear. The young need their sleep.'

Brian advanced a few steps, then spoke in a carefully controlled voice.

'I am going to ask you for the last time, Mrs Brown, or

whatever your name is – what have you done with Rosemary?'

She looked up and shook her head in sad reproof.

'Threats! How unwise. A sparrow should never threaten an eagle. It is so futile and such a waste of time.'

Mrs Brown carefully placed her work-basket on the floor, then snapped in a surprisingly firm voice: 'Carlo!'

There came, from somewhere to Brian's rear, a low, deep growl. Such a menacing sound might have issued from the throat of a large dog whose mistress had been threatened, or a she-wolf protecting her young, but when the young man spun round, he saw Carlo standing a few feet away. The man had his head tilted to one side and his large, yellow teeth were bared as he growled again. His stance was grotesque. He was leaning forward slightly as though preparing to spring and his fingers were curved, so that with their long, pointed nails, they looked uncannily like talons; his cheeks seemed to have shrunk and his black hair lay back over his narrow skull like a sleek, ebony mane.

'Will you believe me?' Mrs Brown said, and her voice was less harsh – much younger. 'I have only to say one word and your windpipe will be hanging down your shirt-front.'

'You are mad.' Brian backed slowly away and Carlo moved forward, matching him step for step. 'You are both mad.'

'You mean,' Mrs Brown came round and joined Carlo, 'we are not normal by your standards. That much I grant you. Sanity is only a form of madness favoured by the majority. But I think the time has come for you to meet truth, since you are so eager to make her acquaintance.'

'I only want to find Rosemary, then get out of here,' Brian said.

'Find your little friend? Perhaps. Leave here? Ah ... ' Mrs Brown looked thoughtful. 'That is another matter. But come, there is much for you to see, and please, no heroics. Carlo is on the turn. He is apt to be a little touchy when the moon is full.'

They filed out into the hall, Mrs Brown leading the way with Brian following and the grim Carlo bringing up the rear. To the right of a great staircase was a black door and this Mrs Brown unlocked, then entered the room beyond, where she proceeded to light a lamp from Brian's candle.

The light crept outwards in ever-increasing cirlces as she turned up the wick, revealing oak-panelled walls and a cobweb-festooned ceiling. The room was bare, except for the portrait hanging over a dirt-grimed marble fireplace. To this the young man's eyes were drawn like a pin to a magnet.

The background was jet-black and the face corpse-white; the large black eyes glared an intense hatred for all living things and the thin-lipped mouth was shut tight, but so cunningly had the portrait been painted that Brian had the feeling it might open at any moment.

'My late husband,' Mrs Brown stated, 'was a partaker of blood.'

The statement did not invite comment and Brian made none.

'It must be the best part of five hundred years since they came down from the village,' Mrs Brown continued. 'Chanting priests looking like black ravens, mewing peasants huddled together like frightened sheep. I recall it was night and the mists shrouded the moors and swirled about their thrice-accursed cross as though it wished to protect us from the menace it represented.'

She paused and Brian realised that she looked much younger. The face was filling out, the shoulders were no longer bowed.

'They did not consider I was of great importance,' Mrs Brown went on, 'so I was merely tied to a tree and flogged, thereby providing entertainment for the herd of human cattle who liked nothing better than to see a woman writhe under the lash. But him ... They dug a hole, and laid him flat, having bound his body in cords that were sealed with the dreaded sign. Then they drove a stake though his heart ... Fools.'

She glared at Brian and clenched her small fists.

'They left him for dead. Dead! His brain still lived. The blood was only symbolic, it was the vital essence we needed – still need: the force that makes the soul reach out for the stars, the hammer that can create beauty out of black depravity.'

She went over to the portrait and stroked the white, cruel face with hands that had become long and slender.

'When they buried his beautiful body they planted a seed,

and from that seed grew the house. A projection of himself.'

'I don't believe you.' Brian shook his head. 'I won't – can't believe you.'

'No!' She laughed and Carlo howled. 'Then feel the walls. They are warm, flesh of his flesh. Moist. The body fluids seep out when he is aroused. 'Look, the mouth. When I open the lips, food pops in. Succulent, living food and we all benefit. I, Carlo, who sprang from the old people – I still let him roam the moors when the moon is full – and, of course, He. The House. He needs all the sweet essence He can get. He sleeps after meat and no longer moans. I do not like to hear Him moan.'

'Where is Rosemary?' Brian asked again and knew what must follow.

'She passed through the lips an hour since.' Mrs Brown laughed very softly and Carlo made a whining sound. 'Now, if you would find her, there is not really much alternative. You must follow her through the great intestines, down into the mighty bowels. Wander and cry out, trudge on and on, until at last your will is broken and He can take from you what He needs.'

'You want me to go through those doors?' Brian asked, and there was a glimmer of hope. 'Then go wandering through the corridors of an empty house? When I find Rosemary, we will break out.'

The woman smiled as she motioned to Carlo.

'Part the lips, Carlo.'

The man, if indeed that which crept forward was a man, silently obeyed; the great doors groaned as they swung inwards and Brian saw a murky passage, lined with green tinted walls. A warm, sweet, cloying odour made his stomach heave and he drew back.

'She's waiting for you,' Mrs Brown said softly, 'and she must be very frightened wandering through the labyrinth, not exactly alone, but I doubt if she will appreciate the company. Most of them will be well digested by now.'

Carlo was waiting, his hand on the handle of one door; his eyes were those of a hungry wolf who sees his prey about to be devoured by a lion. Brian, without a sideways glance, passed through the entrance and the doors slammed to behind him.

*

There were no stairs. The corridors sometimes sloped upwards, at others they spiralled down; there were stretches when the floor was comparatively level, but the corridors were never straight for long. They twisted, crossed other passages, suddenly split, leaving the wanderer with a choice of three or more openings; occasionally they came to a blank end, forcing him to retrace his footsteps. Light was provided by an eerie greenish glow radiating from the walls and ceiling and sometimes this light pulsated, suggesting it originated from some form of decay.

Brian stumbled onwards, shouting Rosemary's name, and his echo mocked him, went racing on ahead until it became a faraway voice calling back along the avenues of time. Once he stumbled and fell against the wall. Instantly, the moist, green surface contracted under his weight and there was an obscene sucking sound when he pulled himself free. A portion of his shirt sleeve remained stuck to the wall and there was a red mark on his arm.

When he had been walking for some thirty minutes he came upon the window passage. There was no other word to describe it, for one wall was lined with windows, each one set about six feet apart, and he gave a little cry of joy, certain this was the place from which he and Rosemary could make their escape. Then he saw – them. Before each window stood one, occasionally two, forms – hideously thin, scarecrow figures that pawed at the window panes with clawlike fingers and emitted little animal whimpers.

Brian approached the first window and gave a quick glance through the grimy panes. He was two floors, if that was the right expression, up, and saw the lawn then, further out, the moors, all bathed in brilliant moonlight. Even as he watched, a great hound went leaping across the lawn. It cleared the low wall in a single leap, then streaked out across the moor. Something touched Brian's arm and he spun round to face one of the creatures that had silently crept along from the next window. He saw at close quarters the skeleton face covered with brown, wrinkled skin, and the vacant blue eyes that stared up at him with mute, suffering appeal. He judged the man to have been a tramp, or possibly a gypsy, for he wore the remnants of a red shirt and brown corduroy trousers. The claw-hands plucked feebly at his arm, the mouth opened, revealing toothless gums, and a hoarse whisper seeped out.

'The old cow said come in.'

'How long have you been here?' Brian asked, uncomfortably aware that a number of other grotesque bundles of rag and bones were leaving their posts by the windows and slithering on naked feet towards him. The whisper came again.

'The old cow said come in.'

'Have you seen a young girl?' Brian shouted. 'Have any of you seen a girl?'

The man tried to grip his arm, but there was no strength left in the wasted frame and he could only repeat the single phrase:

'The old cow said come in.'

They were all clustered round him. Three bore some resemblance to women, although their hair had fallen out, and one, a tall, beanstalk of a creature, kept mumbling: 'Pretty boy,' while she tried unsuccessfully to fasten her gums into his neck.

'Break the windows!' Brian shouted, pushing them away as gently as he could. 'Listen, break the windows, then I'll be able to climb down and fetch help.'

'The old cow said come in.' The man could only repeat over and over the six ominous words, and a wizened, awful thing, no higher than a child, kept muttering: 'Meat,' as it tried to fasten its mouth on Brian's right hand.

Unreasoning terror made him strike the creature full in the face and it went crashing back against the wall. Instantly, the green surface bent inwards and a deep sigh ran through the house, making the ghastly pack go slithering along the corridor, their remaining spark of intelligence having presumably warned them this sound was something to be feared. The small, child-size figure was left, stuck to the wall like a fly on gummed paper, and, as the green light pulsated the creature jerked in unison.

Brian pulled off one of his shoes and smashed the heel against the nearest window-pane. He might just as well have struck a slab of solid rock for all the impression he made, and at last he gave up and continued his search for Rosemary. After an hour of trudging wearily along green-tinted passages, he had no idea of how far he had travelled, or if indeed he was just going round in a perpetual circle. He found himself dragging his feet, making the same hesitant, slithering footsteps that had so alarmed him in his bedroom, centuries ago.

The corridors were never silent, for there were always cries, usually some way off, and a strange thudding sound which came into being when the green light pulsated, but these off-stage noises became as a murmur when the scream rang out. It was a cry of despair, a call for help, a fear-born prayer, and at once Brian knew who had screamed. He shouted Rosemary's name as he broke into a run, terrified lest he be unable to reach her, at the same time in dread of what he might find. Had she not screamed again he would doubtlessly have taken the wrong passage, but when the second shriek rang out he ran towards the sound and presently came to a kind of circular hall. They were clinging to her like leeches to a drowning horse. Their skeleton hands were tearing her dress, their toothless mouths fouled her flesh, and all the while they squealed like a herd of hungry pigs. He pulled them away and the soulless bodies went hurtling back against vibrating walls; bones snapped like frost-crisp twigs and despairing whimpers rose to an unholy chorus.

He took Rosemary in his arms and she clung to him as though he were life itself, clutching his shoulders in a terrified grip while she cried like a lost child. He murmured soft, unintelligble words, trying to reassure himself as much as her, then screamed at the pack who were again slowly moving in.

'Don't you understand, this is not real. It's the projection of a mad brain. A crazy nightmare. Try to find a way out.'

It is doubtful if they heard, let alone understood what he was saying, and those that could still move were edging their way forward like rats whose hunger is greater than their fear.

'Can you walk?' he asked Rosemary and the girl nodded.

'Good, then we must make our way downwards. The woman's apartment is on the ground floor and our only hope is to batter those doors in and escape across the lawn.'

'It's impossible.' Rosemary was clinging to his arm and they were leaving the creatures behind. 'This place is a labyrinth. We will wander round and round these corridors until we drop.'

'Nonsense.' He spoke sharply. 'The house can't be all that big and we are young and fit. So long as we go down, we're bound to find the doors.'

This was easier said than done. Many corridors sloped down, only to slant up again, but presently they came out into a window passage and found they were somewhere at the rear of the house, but only one floor up.

'Now,' Brian kissed Rosemary. 'Only one more slope to go and we're there.'

'But we're the wrong side of the house,' Rosemary complained, 'and even if we find the doors, how are you going to break through them?'

'One step at a time. Let's find them first, then, maybe, I'll use you as a battering ram.'

It took an hour to find the next downward slope and then only after they had retraced their steps several times, but at last they were moving downwards. Rosemary shivered.

'It's getting colder.'

'Yes, and that damned stink is becoming more pronounced. But never mind, we'll soon be there.'

They went steadily downwards for another five minutes and then Rosemary began to cry.

'Brian, I can't go on much longer. Surely we've passed the ground floor ages ago? And there's something awful down here. I can feel it.'

'It can't be more awful than what's up above,' he retorted grimly. 'We must go on. There's no turning back unless you want to finish up a zombie.'

'Zombie!' She repeated dully.

'What did you imagine those things were, back there? They died long ago and only keep going because the house gives them a sort of half life. Mrs Brown and Carlo appear to be better provided for, but they died centuries ago.'

'I can't believe all this.' Rosemary shuddered. 'How can a place like this exist in the twentieth century?'

'It doesn't. I should imagine we stumbled across the house at the right, or in our case, the wrong time. I suppose you might call it a time-trap.'

'I don't know what you are talking about,' Rosemary said, then added, 'I very rarely do.'

The passage was becoming steeper, spiralling round and sloping down until they had difficulty in remaining upright. Then the floor levelled out and after a space of about six feet came to an end.

'Earth.' Brian felt the termination wall. 'Good, honest earth.'

'Earth,' Rosemary repeated. 'So what?'

Brian raised his eyes ceilingwards and then spoke in a carefully controlled voice. 'So far we have been walking on a floor and between walls that are constructed of something very nasty. Right? Now we are facing a wall built or shovelled into place – I don't care – of plain, down to earth – earth. Got it?'

Rosemary nodded. 'Yes, so we have got down to the house foundations. But I thought we were looking for the doors.'

Brian gripped her shoulders.

'Say that again.'

'Say what again? Look, you're hurting me.'

He shook her gently. 'The first bit.'

She thought for a moment. 'So we have got down to the house foundations. What's so important about that?'

He released her and went up close to the wall, where he stood for a few minutes examining its surface, then he came back and tilted her chin up so she was looking directly into his eyes.

'Will you try to be very, very brave?'

Fear came rushing back and she shivered.

'Why?'

'Because I am going to break down that wall.' He spoke very slowly. 'And on the other side we may find something very nasty indeed.'

She did not move her head, only continued to gaze up into his eyes.

'Isn't there any other way?' she whispered.

He shook his head.

'None. None whatsoever.'

There was a minute of complete silence, then:

'What are you going to use as a shovel?'

He laughed and went back to the wall which he pounded with his fist.

'I could say you have a point there, but I won't. Let's take an inventory. What have we that is pick and shovel-worthy? Our hands, of course. Shoes? Maybe.' He felt in his pocket and produced a bunch of keys and a penknife. 'This might start things going, then I can pull the loose stuff out with my hands.'

He sank the penknife blade into the soft, moist earth and traced the rough outline of a door, then he began to deepen the edges, digging out little lumps of earth that fell to the ground like gobbets of chewed meat. Brian then removed his shoes and used the heels to claw out a jagged hole.

'If I can work my way through,' he explained, 'it should be an easy matter to pull the entire thing down.'

He dug steadily for another five minutes, then a glimmer of light appeared and, after a final effort, he was able to look through an opening roughly six inches in diameter.

'What can you see?' Rosemary asked, her tone suggesting she would rather not know.

'It seems to be some kind of large cave and it's lit up with that green light, just like the passages. I can see hunks of rock lying about, but not much else. Well, here goes.'

He thrust his right hand through the aperture, curled his fingers round the inner wall and pulled. A large chunk came away, then he began to work with both hands, pulling, clawing, and the entire wall came tumbling down. He wiped his hands on already stained trousers, then put on his shoes.

'Now,' he said, 'for the moment of truth.'

They were in a rough, circular cavern; it was perhaps twenty feet in diameter and an equal distance in height. Loose lumps of rock littered the floor, but there was no sign of anyone – alive or dead – and Brian gave a prolonged sigh of relief.

'I don't know what I expected to see, but thank heavens, I don't see it. Now, we must start looking for a way out. I'll go round the walls, you examine the floor. Never know, there might be a hole going down still further.'

He turned his attention to the irregular walls, leaving Rosemary to wander miserably among the large rocks and boulders that formed a kind of fence round the centre of the cavern. He looked upwards and saw, some twenty feet from the ground, a fairly large hole. Deciding it would be worth investigating, he began to ascend the wall and found the task easier than he had supposed, for projecting rocks made excellent footholds. In a few minutes he had reached his objective. The hole was in fact a small cave that was about seven feet high and five across, but alas there was no exit.

He was about to descend and continue his search elsewhere when Rosemary screamed. Never before had he realised a human throat was capable of expressing such abject terror. Shriek after shriek rang out and re-echoed against the walls, until it seemed an army of banshees were forecasting a million deaths. He looked down and saw the girl standing just inside the fence of stones looking down at something he could not see; her eyes were dilated and seemed frozen into an expression of indescribable horror.

Brian scrambled down the wall and ran over to her; when he laid hands on her shoulders she flinched as though his touch were a branding iron, then her final shriek was cut off and she slid silently to the floor.

A few feet away there was a slight indentation, a shallow hole, and he experienced a terrifying urge not to look into it, but he knew he must, if for no other reason than a strange, compelling curiosity.

He dragged Rosemary well back and left her lying against one wall, then he returned, creeping forward very slowly, walking on tip-toe. At last he was on the brink of hell. He looked down.

Horror ran up his body in cold waves; it left an icy lump in his stomach and he wanted to be sick only he had not the strength. He had to stare down, concentrate all his senses and try to believe.

The head bore a resemblance to the portrait in Mrs Brown's ante-room; it was dead-white, bloated, suggesting an excess of nourishment consumed over a very long period. The hair was at least six feet in length and was spread out over the loose rock like a monstrous shroud. But the torso and arms grew out of the ground. The shoulders and part of the forearms were flesh, but further down the white skin assumed a greyish colour and, lower still, gradually merged into solid rock. Most horrifying of all was the profusion of fat, greenish, tubelike growths that sprouted out from under forearms and neck and, so far as Brian could see, the whole of the back. Obscene roots spreading out in every direction until they disappeared into the black earth, writhing and pulsating, carrying the vital fluid that circulated round the house.

The eyes were closed, but the face moved. The thin lips grimaced, creating temporary furrows in the flabby fat. Brian withdrew from the hole – the grave – and at last his stomach had its way and allowed him to be violently sick. By the time he returned to Rosemary, he felt old and drained of strength. She was just returning to consciousness and he smoothed back her hair.

'Are you fit enough to talk?' he asked.

She gave a little strangled gasp.

'That ... that thing ... '

'Yes, I know. Now listen. I am going to take you up there.' He pointed to the cave set high up on the opposite wall. 'You'll be all right up there while I do what must be done.'

'I don't understand.' She shook her head. 'What must you do?'

'Mrs Brown told me her husband was a partaker of blood. In other words, a vampire, and centuries ago the local lads did the traditional things and drove a stake through his heart. She said something else. It wasn't his body they should have destroyed, but his brain. Don't you see? This house, the entire set-up, is a nightmare produced by a monstrous intelligence?'

'I'll believe anything.' Rosemary got to her feet. 'Just get me out of here. I'd rather walk the passages than spend another minute with that ... thing.'

'No.' He shook his head. 'I must destroy the brain. The only point is, when I do ... ' He looked round the cavern, then over to the entrance of the green-walled passage. ' ... anything may happen.'

'What about you?' she asked.

'So soon as the job is finished, I'll join you.'

He might have added, 'If I can,' but instead guided Rosemary to the wall and assisted her up to the cave.

'Now,' he instructed, 'stay well back and don't, in any circumstances, so much as put your nose outside. Understand?'

'God, I'm petrified,' she said.

'Don't let it get around,' he nodded grimly, 'but so am I.'

He came back to the hole like a released spirit returning to hell. As he drew nearer, the terror grew until it required a desperate effort to raise one foot and put it down before the other. Only the memory of Rosemary up there in the cave kept his spark of courage alive. At last he again gazed down at that horrible growth; it groaned and the sound raced round the cavern and up through the house. The face grimaced and twitched, while the green tubes writhed like a nest of gorged worms. Brian selected a rock which was a little larger than the bloated head and, gripping it in both hands, prepared to hurl it down. He had tensed his muscles, and was turning slightly to one side, when the eyelids flicked back and he was staring into two pools of black hate.

The shock was so intense he automatically slackened his grip and the rock slid from his fingers and went crashing down somewhere behind him. The mouth opened and a vibrant whisper went racing up through the house.

'Elizabeth … Carlo … '

The words came out slowly, rather like a series of intelligible sighs, but from all around, from the walls, the floor, the high roof – never from the moving lips.

'Would … you … destroy … that … which … you do … not … understand?'

Brian was fumbling for the rock, but he paused and the whispering voice went on.

'I … must … continue … to … be … I … must … grow … fill … the … universe … consume … take … strength … '

A padding of fast-running paws came from the passage entrance and a woman's voice was calling out.

'Petros, drink of his essence … will him into walking death.'

There was a hint of fear in the terrible eyes. The whispering voice again ran through the house.

'He … is … an … unbeliever … he … is … the … young … of … a … new … age … why … did … you … let … him … through … ?'

The great dog leapt over the loose earth and emerged from the passageway; it was black as midnight, like a solid shadow newly escaped from a wall, and it padded round the cavern before jumping up on to a boulder and preparing to leap. Brian hurled a rock at it and struck the broad, black snout. The beast howled and fell back as Mrs Brown spoke from the entrance.

'You will not keep that up for long. Carlo cannot be killed by the likes of you.'

She had been transformed. The once white hair was now a rich auburn, the face was as young as today, but the glorious eyes reflected the evil of a million yesterdays. She wore a black evening dress that left her arms and back bare and Brian could only stare at her, forgetting that which lay behind him and Rosemary, up in the cave. All he could see was white flesh and inviting eyes.

'Come away,' the low, husky voice said. 'Leave Petros to his dream. He cannot harm you and it would be such a waste if Carlo were to rip your nice body to shreds. Think of what I can offer. An eternity of bliss. A million lifetimes of pleasure. Come.'

He took one step forward, then another, and it seemed he was walking into a forbidden dream; all the secret desires that up to that moment he had not realised existed flared up and became exciting possibilities. Then, just as he was about to surrender, go running to her like a child to a beautiful toy, her voice lashed across his consciousness.

'Carlo … now.'

The dog came snarling over the rocks and Brian fell back, suddenly fully aware of the pending danger. He snatched up a piece of jagged rock and threw it at the oncoming beast. He hit it just above the right ear, then began to hurl stones as fast as he could pick them up. The dog leapt from side to side, snarling with pain and rage, but Brian realised it was coming forward more than it retreated and knew a few minutes, at the most, must elapse before he felt those fangs at his throat. By chance his hands closed round the original small boulder – and it was then he understood what must be done.

He raised the rock high above his head, made as though to hurl it at the dog, which momentarily recoiled, then threw it back – straight at the head of Petros.

The house shrieked. One long-drawn-out scream and the dog was no longer there; instead, Carlo ran towards his mistress, making plaintive, guttural cries, before sinking down before her, plucking frantically at the hem of her black dress.

Brian looked back and down into the hole and saw that the head was shattered and what remained of the flesh was turning black. The green tubes were now only streaks of deflated tissue and all the life-giving fluid no longer flowed up into the body of the house. From up above came a deep rumbling sound and a great splintering, as though a mountain of rocks were grinding together. Brian ran towards the far wall and quickly scrambling up into the cave, found Rosemary waiting to welcome him with outstretched arms.

'Keep down,' he warned. 'All hell is going to break loose at any moment.'

They lay face down upon the floor, and Brian had to raise his head to see the final act. The green light was fading, but before it went he had a last glimpse of the woman staring blankly at the place where Petros had lain. She was patting Carlo's head. Then the ceiling came down and for a while there was only darkness filled with a mighty rumbling and crashing of falling rock. Fantasy tumbling down into the pit of reality. Time passed and the air cleared as the dust settled and presently, like a glimmer of hope in the valley of despair, a beam of light struck the entrance to the cave. Brian looked out, then up. Twenty feet above was a patch of blue sky.

*

They came up from the pit, bruised, clothes torn, but happy to be alive. They trudged hand-in-hand out across the moors and after a while looked back to see a pile of rocks that, at this distance, could have been mistaken for a ruined house.

'We will never talk about this to anyone,' Brain said. 'One does not talk about one's nightmares. They are so ridiculous in the light of day.'

Rosemary nodded. 'We slept. We dreamed. Now we are awake.'

They walked on. Two figures that distance diminished until they became minute specks on a distant horizon. Then they were gone.

The early morning breeze caressed the summer grass, hare-bells smiled up at a benign sky and a pair of rabbits played hide and seek among the fallen rocks. To all outward appearances the moors were at peace.

Then a rabbit screamed and a stoat raised blood-dripping jaws.

VI

A Descent Into The Maelström

Edgar Allan Poe

We had now reached the summit of the loftiest crag. For some minutes the old man seemed too much exhausted to speak.

'Not long ago,' he said at length, 'and I could have guided you on this route as well as the youngest of my sons; but, about three years past, there happened to me an event such as never happened before to mortal man – or at least such as no man ever survived to tell of – and the six hours of deadly terror which I then endured have broken me up body and soul. You suppose me a *very* old man – but I am not. It took less than a single day to change these hairs from a jetty black to white, to weaken my limbs, and to unstring my nerves, so that I tremble at the least exertion, and am frightened at a shadow. Do you know I can scarcely look over this little cliff without getting giddy?'

The 'little cliff,' upon whose edge he had so carelessly thrown himself to rest that the weightier portion of his body hung over it, while he was only kept from falling by the tenure of his elbow on its extreme and slippery edge – this 'little cliff' arose, a sheer unobstructed precipice of black shining rock, some fifteen or sixteen hundred feet from the world of crags beneath us. Nothing would have tempted me to within half a dozen yards of its brink. In truth, so deeply was I excited by the perilous position of my companion, that I fell at full length upon the ground, clung to the shrubs around me, and dared not even glance upwards at the sky – while I struggled in vain to divest myself of the idea that the very foundations of the mountain were in danger from the fury of the winds. It was long before I could reason myself into sufficient courage to sit up and look out into the distance.

'You must get over these fancies,' said the guide, 'for I have brought you here that you might have the best possible view of the scene of that event I mentioned – and to tell you the whole story with the spot just under your eye.

'We are now,' he continued, in that particularizing manner which distinguished him – 'we are now close upon the Norwegian coast – in the sixty-eighth degree of latitude – in the great province of Nordland – and in the dreary district of Lofoden. The mountain upon whose top we sit is Helseggen, the Cloudy. Now raise yourself up a little higher – hold on to the grass if you feel giddy – so – and look out, beyond the belt of vapour beneath us, into the sea.'

I looked dizzily, and beheld a wide expanse of ocean, whose waters wore so inky a hue as to bring at once to my mind the Nubian geographer's account of the *Mare Tenebrarum*. A panorama more deplorably desolate no human imagination can conceive. To the right and left, as far as the eye could reach, there lay outstretched, like ramparts of the world, lines of horridly black and beetling cliff, whose character of gloom was but the more forcibly illustrated by the surf which reared high up against its white and ghastly crest, howling and shrieking for ever. Just opposite the promontory upon whose apex we were placed, and at a distance of some five or six miles out at sea, there was visible a small, bleak-looking island; or, more properly, its position was discernible through the wilderness of wild surge in which it was enveloped. About two miles nearer the land, arose another of smaller size, hideously craggy and barren, and encompassed at various intervals by a cluster of dark rocks.

The appearance of the ocean, in the space between the more distant island and the shore, had something very unusual about it. Although, at the time, so strong a gale was blowing landward that a brig in the remote offing lay to under a double-reefed trysail, and constantly plunged her whole hull out of sight, still there was here nothing like a regular swell, but only a short, quick, angry cross dashing of water in every direction – as well in the teeth of the wind as otherwise. Of foam there was little except in the immediate vicinity of the rocks.

'The island in the distance,' resumed the old man, 'is called by the Norwegians Vurrgh. The one midway is Moskoe. That a mile to the northward is Ambaaren. Yonder are Islesen, Hotholm, Keildhelm, Suarven and Buckholm. Farther off – between Moskoe and Vurrgh – are Otterholm, Flimen, Sandflesen and Stockholm. These are the true names of the places – but why it has been thought necessary to name them at all is more than either you or I can understand. Do you hear anything? Do you see any change in the water?'

We had now been about ten minutes upon the top of Helseggen, to which we had ascended from the interior of Lofoden, so that we had caught no glimpse of the sea until it had burst upon us from the summit. As the old man spoke, I became aware of a loud and gradually increasing sound, like the moaning of a vast herd of buffaloes upon an American prairie; and at the same moment I perceived that what seamen term the *chopping* character of the ocean beneath us was rapidly changing into a current which set to the eastward. Even while I gazed, this current acquired a monstrous velocity. Each moment added to its speed – to its headlong impetuosity. In five minutes the whole sea, as far as Vurrgh, was lashed into ungovernable fury; but it was between Moskoe and the coast that the main uproar held its sway. Here the vast bed of the waters, seamed and scarred into a thousand conflicting channels, burst suddenly into frenzied convulsion – heaving, boiling, hissing – gyrating in gigantic and innumerable vortices, and all whirling and plunging on to the eastward with a rapidity which water never elsewhere assumes, except in precipitous descents.

In a few minutes more, there came over the sea another radical alteration. The general surface grew somewhat more smooth, and the whirlpools, one by one, disappeared, while prodigious streaks of foam became apparent where none had been seen before. These streaks, at length, spreading out to a great distance, and entering into combination, took unto themselves the gyratory motion of the subsided vortices, and seemed to form the germ of another more vast. Suddenly – very suddenly – this assumed a distinct and definite existence, in a circle of more than a mile in diameter. The edge of the whirl was represented by a broad belt of gleaming spray; but no particle of this slipped into the mouth of the terrific funnel, whose interior, as far as the eye could fathom it, was a smooth, shining and jet-black wall of water, inclined to the horizon at an angle of some forty-five degrees, speeding dizzily round and round with a swaying and sweltering motion, and sending forth to the winds an appalling voice, half shriek, half roar, such as not even the mighty cataract of Niagara ever lifts up in its agony to heaven.

The mountain trembled to its very base, and the rock rocked. I threw myself upon my face, and clung to the scant herbage in an excess of nervous agitation.

'This,' said I at length to the old man, 'this *can* be nothing else than the great whirlpool of the Maelström.'

'So it is sometimes termed,' said he. 'We Norwegians call it the Moskoe-ström, from the island of Moskoe in the midway.'

The ordinary accounts of this vortex had by no means prepared me for what I saw. That of Jonas Ramus, which is perhaps the most circumstantial of any, cannot impart the faintest conception either of the magnificence, or of the horror of the scene – or of the wild bewildering sense of *the novel* which confounds the beholder. I am not sure from what point of view the writer in question surveyed it, nor at what time; but it could neither have been from the summit of Helseggen, nor during a storm. There are some passages of his description, nevertheless, which may be quoted for their details, although their effect is exceedingly feeble in conveying an impression of the spectacle.

'Between Lofoden and Moskoe,' he says 'the depth of the water is between thirty-six and forty fathoms; but on the other side, towards Ver (Vurrgh), this depth decreases so as not to afford a convenient passage for a vessel, without the risk of splitting on the rocks, which happens even in the calmest weather. When it is flood, the stream runs up the country between Lofoden and Moskoe with a boisterous rapidity; but the roar of its impetuous ebb to the sea is scarce equalled by the loudest and most dreadful cataracts; the noise being heard several leagues off, and the vortices or pits are of such an extent and depth, that if a ship comes within its attraction, it is inevitably absorbed and carried down to the bottom, and there beat to pieces against the rocks; and when the water relaxes, the fragments thereof are thrown up again. But these intervals of tranquillity are only at the turn of the ebb and flood, and in calm weather, and last but a quarter of an hour, its violence gradually returning. When the stream is most boisterous, and its fury heightened by a storm, it is dangerous to come within a Norway mile of it. Boats, yachts, and ships have been carried away by not guarding against it before they were within its reach. It likewise happens frequently that whales come too near the stream, and are overpowered by its violence; and then it is impossible to describe their howlings and bellowings in their fruitless struggles to disengage themselves. A bear, once attempting to swim from Lofoden to Moskoe, was caught by the stream and borne down, while he roared terribly, so as to be heard on shore. Large stocks of firs and pine trees, after being absorbed by the current, rise again broken and torn to such a degree as if bristles grew upon them. This plainly shows the bottom to consist of craggy rocks, among which they are whirled to and fro. This stream is regulated by the flux and reflux of the sea – it being constantly high and low water every six hours. In the year 1645, early in the morning of Sexagesima Sunday, it raged with such noise and impetuosity that the very stones of the houses on the coast fell to the ground.'

In regard to the depth of the water, I could not see how this could have been ascertained at all in the immediate vicinity of the vortex. The 'forty fathoms' must have reference only to portions of the channel close upon the shore either of Moskoe or Lofoden. The depth in the centre of the Moskoe-ström must be immeasurably greater; and no better proof of this fact is necessary than can be obtained from even the sidelong glance into the abyss of the whirl which may be had from the highest crag of Helseggen. Looking down from this pinnacle upon the howling Phlegethon below, I could not help smiling at the simplicity with which the honest Jonas Ramus records, as a matter difficult of belief, the anecdotes of the whales and the bears; for it appeared to me, in fact, a self-evident thing, that the largest ships of the line in existence, coming within the influence of that deadly attraction, could resist it as little as a feather the hurricane, and must disappear bodily and at once.

The attempts to account for the phenomenon – some of which, I remember, seemed to me sufficiently plausible in perusal – now wore a very different and unsatisfactory aspect. The idea generally received is that this, as well as three small vortices among the Ferroe islands, 'have no other cause than the collision of waves rising and falling, at flux and reflux, against a ridge of rocks and shelves, which confines the water so that it precipitates itself like a cataract, and thus the higher the flood rises, the deeper must the fall be; and the natural result of all is a whirlpool or vortex, the prodigious suction of which is sufficiently known by lesser experiments.' These are the words of the *Encyclopaedia Britannica*. Kircher and others imagine that in the centre of the channel of the Maelström is an abyss penetrating the globe, and issuing in some very remote part – the gulf of Bothnia being somewhat decidedly named in one instance. This opinion, idle in itself, was the one to which, as I gazed, my imagination most readily assented; and, mentioning it to the guide, I was rather surprised to hear him say that, although it was the view almost universally entertained of the subject by the Norwegians, it nevertheless was not his own. As to the former notion, he confessed his inability to comprehend it; and here I agreed with him – for, however conclusive on paper, it becomes altogether unintelligible, and even absurd, amid the thunder of the abyss.

'You have had a good look at the whirl now,' said the old man; 'and if you will creep round this crag, so as to get in its lee, and deaden the roar of the water, I will tell you a story that will convince you I ought to know something of the Moskoe-ström.'

I placed myself as desired, and he proceeded:

'Myself and my two brothers once owned a schooner-rigged smack of about seventy tons burthen, with which we were in the habit of fishing among the islands beyond Moskoe, nearly to Vurrgh. In all violent eddies at sea there is good fishing, at proper opportunites, if one has only the courage to attempt it;

but among the whole of the Lofoden coastmen, we three were the only ones who made a regular business of going out to the islands, as I tell you. The usual grounds are a great way lower down to the southward. There fish can be got at all hours, without much risk, and therefore these places are preferred. The choice spots over here among the rocks, however, not only yield the finest variety, but in far greater abundance; so that we often got in a single day what the more timid of the craft could not scrape together in a week. In fact, we made it a matter of desperate speculation – the risk of life standing instead of labour, and courage answering for capital.

'We kept the smack in a cove about five miles higher up the coast than this; and it was our practice, in fine weather, to take advantage of the fifteen minutes' slack to push across the main channel of the Moskoe-ström, far above the pool, and then drop down upon anchorage somewhere near Otterholm, or Sandflesen, where the eddies are not so violent as elsewhere. Here we used to remain until nearly time for slack-water again, when we weighed and made for home. We never set out upon this expedition without a steady side wind for going and coming – one that we felt sure would not fail us before our return – and we seldom made a miscalculation upon this point. Twice, during six years, we were forced to stay all night at anchor, on account of a dead calm, which is a rare thing indeed just about here; and once we had to remain on the grounds nearly a week, starving to death, owing to a gale which blew up shortly after our arrival, and made the channel too boisterous to be thought of. Upon this occasion we should have been driven out to sea in spite of everything (for the whirlpools threw us round and round so violently that at length we fouled our anchor and dragged it) if it had not been that we drifted into one of the innumerable cross-currents – here to-day and gone to-morrow – which drove us under the lee of Flimen, where, by good luck, we brought up.

'I could not tell you the twentieth part of the difficulties we encountered "on the ground" – it is a bad spot to be in, even in good weather – but we make shift always to run the gauntlet of the Moskoe-ström itself without accident; although at times my heart has been in my mouth when we happened to be a minute or so behind or before the slack. The wind sometimes was not as strong as we thought it at starting, and then we made rather less way than we could wish, while the current rendered the smack unmanageable. My eldest brother had a son eighteen years old, and I had two stout boys of my own. These would have been of great assistance at such times in using the sweeps, as well as afterward in fishing – but, somehow, although we ran the risk ourselves, we had not the heart to let the young ones get into the danger – for, after all said and done, it *was* a horrible danger, and that is the truth.

'It is now within a few days of three years since what I am going to tell you occurred. It was on the 10th of July, 18 – , a day which the people of this part of the world will never forget – for it was one in which blew the most terrible hurricane that ever came out of the heavens. And yet all the morning, and indeed until late afternoon, there was a gentle and steady breeze from the south-west, while the sun shone brightly, so that the oldest seaman amongst us could not have foreseen what was to follow.

'The three of us – my brothers and myself – had crossed over to the islands about two o'clock p.m., and soon nearly loaded the smack with fine fish, which, we all remarked, were more plentiful that day than we had ever known them. It was just seven *by my watch* when we weighed and started for home, so as to make the worst of the Ström at slack water, which we knew would be at eight.

'We set out with a fresh wind on our starboard quarter, and for some time spanked along at a great rate, never dreaming of danger, for indeed we saw not the slightest reason to apprehend it. All at once we were taken aback by a breeze from over Helseggen. This was most unusual – something that had never happened to us before – and I began to feel a little uneasy, without exactly knowing why. We put the boat on the wind, but could make no headway at all for the eddies, and I was upon the point of proposing to return to the anchorage when, looking astern, we saw the whole horizon covered with a singular copper-coloured cloud that rose with the most amazing velocity.

'In the meantime the breeze that had headed us off fell away, and we were dead becalmed, drifting about in every direction. This state of things, however, did not last long enough to give us time to think about it. In less than a minute the storm was upon us – in less than two the sky was entirely overcast – and what with this and the driving spray, it became suddenly so dark that we could not see each other in the smack.

'Such a hurricane as then blew it is folly to attempt describing. The oldest seaman in Norway never experienced anything like it. We had let our sails go by the run before it cleverly took us; but, at the first puff, both our masts went by the board as if they had been sawed off – the mainmast taking with it my youngest brother, who had lashed himself to it for safety.

'Our boat was the lightest feather of a thing that had ever sat upon water. It had a complete flush deck, with only a small hatch near the bow, and this hatch it had always been our custom to batten down when about to cross the Ström, by way of precaution against the chopping seas. But for this circumstance we should have foundered at once – for we lay entirely buried for some moments. How my elder brother escaped destruction I cannot say, for I never had an opportunity of ascertaining. For my part, as soon as I had let the foresail run, I threw myself flat on deck, with my feet against the narrow gunwale of the bow, and with my hands grasping a ring-bolt near the foot of the foremast. It was mere instinct that prompted me to do this – which was undoubtedly the very best thing I could have done – for I was too much flurried to think.

'For some moments we were completely deluged, as I say, and all this time I held my breath and clung to the bolt. When I could stand it no longer I raised myself upon my knees, still keeping hold with my hands, and thus got my head clear. Presently our little boat gave herself a shake, just as a dog does in coming out of the water, and thus rid herself, in some measure, of the seas. I was now trying to get the better of the stupor that had come over me, and to collect my senses so as to see what was to be done, when I felt somebody grasp my arm. It was my elder brother, and my heart leaped for joy, for I had made sure that he was overboard – but the next moment all this joy was turned into horror – for he put his mouth close to my ear, and screamed out the word "*Moskoe-ström!*"

'No one will ever know what my feelings were at that moment. I shook from head to foot as if I had had the most violent fit of ague. I knew what he meant by that one word well enough – I knew what he wished to make me understand. With the wind that now drove us on, we were bound for the whirl of the Ström, and nothing could save us!

'You perceive that in crossing the Ström *channel* we always went a long way up above the whirl, even in the calmest weather, and then had to wait and watch carefully for the slack – but now we were driving right upon the pool itself, and in such a hurricane as this! "To be sure," I thought, "we shall get there just about the slack – there is some little hope in that" – but in the next moment I cursed myself for being so great a fool as to dream of hope at all. I knew very well that we were doomed, had we been ten times a ninety-gun ship.

'By this time the first fury of the tempest had spent itself, or perhaps we did not feel it so much, as we scudded before it, but at all events the seas, which at first had been kept down by the wind, and lay flat and frothing, now got up into absolute mountains. A singular change, too, had come over the heavens. Around in every direction it was still as black as pitch, but nearly overhead there burst out, all at once, a circular rift of clear sky – as clear as I ever saw – and of a deep bright blue – and through it there blazed forth the full moon with a lustre that I never before knew her to wear. She lit up everything about us with the greatest distinctness – but, oh God, what a scene it was to light up!

'I now made one or two attempts to speak to my brother – but in some manner which I could not understand, the din had so increased that I could not make him hear a single word, although I screamed out at the top of my voice in his ear. Presently he shook his head, looking as pale as death, and held up one of his fingers, as if to say "*listen.*"

'At first I could not make out what he meant – but soon a hideous thought flashed upon me. I dragged my watch from its fob. It was not going. I glanced at its face by the moonlight, and then burst into tears as I flung it far away into the ocean. *It had run down at seven o'clock! We were behind the time of the slack, and the whirl of the Ström was in full fury!*

'When a boat is well built, properly trimmed, and not deep laden, the waves in a strong gale, when she is going large, seem always to slip from beneath her – which appears very strange to a landsman – and this is called *riding*, in sea phrase.

'Well, so far we had ridden the swells very cleverly! but presently a gigantic sea happened to take us right under the counter, and bore us with it as it rose – up – up – as if into the sky. I would not have believed that any wave could rise so high. And then down we came with a sweep, as if I was falling from some lofty mountain-top in a dream. But while we were up I had thrown a quick glance around – and that one glance was sufficient. I saw our exact position in an instant. The Moskoe-ström whirlpool was about a quarter of a mile dead ahead, but no more like the everyday Moskoe-ström than the whirl as you now see it is like a mill-race. If I had not known where we were, and what we had to expect, I should not have recognized the place at all. As it was, I involuntarily closed my eyes in horror. The lids clenched themselves together as if in a spasm.

'It could not have been two minutes afterwards when we suddenly felt the waves subside, and were suddenly enveloped in foam. The boat made a short half-turn to larboard, and then shot off in its new direction like a thunderbolt. At the same moment the roaring noise of the waters was completely drowned in a shrill shriek – such a sound as you might imagine given out by the water-pipes of many thousand steam-vessels, letting off their steam all together. We were now in the belt of surf that always surrounds the whirl! and I thought, of course, that another moment would plunge us into the abyss – down which we could only see indistinctly on account of the amazing velocity with which we were borne along. The boat did not seem to sink into the water at all, but to skim like an air-bubble on the surface of the surge. Her starboard side was next the whirl, and on the larboard arose the world of ocean we had left. It stood like a huge, writhing wall between us and the horizon.

'It may appear strange, but now, when we were in the very

jaws of the gulf, I felt more composed than when we were only approaching it. Having made up my mind to hope no more, I got rid of a great deal of that terror which unmanned me at first. I supposed it was despair that strung my nerves.

'It may look like boasting – but what I tell you is truth – I began to reflect how magnificent a thing it was to die in such a manner, and how foolish it was in me to think of so paltry a consideration as my own individual life, in view of so wonderful a manifestation of God's power. I do believe that I blushed with shame when this idea crossed my mind. After a little while I became possessed with the keenest curiosity about the whirl itself. I positively felt a *wish* to explore its depths, even at the sacrifice I was going to make! and my principal grief was that I should never be able to tell my old companions on shore about the mysteries I should see. These, no doubt, were singular fancies to occupy a man's mind in such extremity – and I have often thought since that the revolutions of the boat around the pool might have rendered me a little light-headed.

'There was another circumstance which tended to restore my self-possession; and this was the cessation of the wind, which could not reach us in our present situation – for, as you saw yourself, the belt of surf is considerably lower than the general bed of the ocean, and this latter now towered above us, a high, black, mountainous ridge. If you have never been at sea in a heavy gale, you can form no idea of the confusion of mind occasioned by the wind and spray together. They blind, deafen, and strangle you, and take away all power of action or reflection. But we were now, in a great measure, rid of these annoyances – just as death-condemned felons in prison are allowed petty indulgences, forbidden them while their doom is yet uncertain.

'How often we made the circuit of the belt it is impossible to say. We careered round and round for perhaps an hour, flying rather than floating, getting gradually more and more into the middle of the surge, and then nearer and nearer to its horrible inner edge. All this time I had never let go of the ring-bolt. My brother was at the stern holding on to an empty water-cask, which had been securely lashed under the coop of the counter, and was the only thing on deck that had not been swept overboard when the gale first took us. As we approached the brink of the pit he let go his hold upon this, and made for the ring, from which, in the agony of his terror, he endeavoured to force my hands, as it was not large enough to afford us both a secure grasp. I never felt deeper grief than when I saw him attempt this act – although I knew he was a madman when he did it – a raving maniac through sheer fright. I did not care, however, to contest the point with him. I knew it could make no difference whether either of us held on at all; so I let him have the bolt and went astern to the cask. This there was no great difficulty in doing; for the smack went round steadily enough, and upon an even keel – only swaying to and fro with the immense swelters of the whirl. Scarcely had I secured myself in my new position, when we gave a wild lurch to starboard, and rushed headlong into the abyss. I muttered a hurried prayer to God, and thought all was over.

'As I felt the sickening sweep of the descent, I had instinctively tightened my hold upon the barrel, and closed my eyes. For some seconds I dared not open them – while I expected instant destruction, and wondered that I was not already in my death-struggles with the water. But moment after moment elapsed. I still lived. The sense of the falling had ceased; and the motion of the vessel seemed much as it had been before, while in the belt of the foam, with the exception that she now lay more along. I took courage and looked once again upon the scene.

'Never shall I forget the sensation of awe, horror, and admiration with which I gazed about me. The boat appeared to be hanging, as if by magic, midway down, upon the interior surface of a funnel, vast in circumference, prodigious in depth, and whose perfectly smooth sides might have been mistaken for ebony, but for the bewildering rapidity with which they spun around, and for the gleaming and ghastly radiance they shot forth, as the rays of the full moon, from that circular rift amid the clouds which I have already described, streamed in a flood of golden glory along the black walls and far away down into the inmost recess of the abyss.

'At first I was too much confused to observe anything accurately. The general burst of terrific grandeur was all that I beheld. When I recovered myself a little, however, my gaze fell instinctively downward. In this direction I was able to obtain an unobstructed view, from the manner in which the smack hung on the inclined surface of the pool. She was quite upon an even keel – that is to say, her deck lay in a plain parallel with that of the water – but this latter sloped at an angle of more than forty-five degrees, so that we seemed to be lying upon our beam ends. I could not help observing, nevertheless, that I had scarcely more difficulty in maintaining my hold and footing in this situation than if we had been upon a dead level; and this, I suppose, was owing to the speed at which we revolved.

'The rays of the moon seemed to search the very bottom of the profound gulf; but still I could make out nothing distinctly, on account of a thick mist in which everything there was enveloped, and over which there hung a magnificent rainbow, like that narrow and tottering bridge which Mussulmen say is the only pathway between Time and Eternity. This mist, or spray, was no doubt occasioned by the clashing of the great walls of the funnel, as they all met together at the bottom – but the yell that went up to the heavens from out of that mist, I dare not attempt to describe.

'Our first slide into the abyss itself, from the belt of foam above, had carried us a great distance down the slope; but our further descent was by no means proportionate. Round and round we swept – not in any uniform movement, but in dizzying swings and jerks that sent us sometimes only a few hundred yards – sometimes nearly the complete circuit of the whirl. Our progress downwards, at each revolution, was slow, but very perceptible.

'Looking about me upon the wide waste of liquid ebony on which we were thus borne, I perceived that our boat was not the only object in the embrace of the whirl. Both above and below us where visible fragments of vessels, large masses of building timber and trunks of trees, with many smaller articles, such as pieces of house furniture, broken boxes, barrels, and staves. I have already described the unnatural curiosity which had taken the place of my original terrors. It appeared to grow upon me as I drew nearer and nearer to my dreadful doom. I now began to watch, with a strange interest, the numerous things that floated in our company. I *must* have been delirious – for I even sought *amusement* in speculating upon the relative velocities of their several descents toward the foam below. "This fir tree," I found myself at one time saying, "will certainly be the next thing that takes the awful plunge and disappears" – and then I was disappointed to find that the wreck of a Dutch merchant ship overtook it and went down before. At length, after making several guesses of this nature, and being deceived in all – this fact – the fact of my invariable miscalculation, set me upon a train of reflection that made my limbs again tremble, and my heart beat heavily once more.

'It was not a new terror that thus affected me, but the dawn of a more exciting *hope*. This hope arose partly from memory, and partly from present observation. I called to mind the great variety of buoyant matter that strewed the coast of Lofoden, having been absorbed and then thrown forth by the Moskoe-ström. By far the greater number of the articles were shattered in the most extraordinary way – so chafed and roughened as to have the appearance of having been stuck full of splinters – but then I distinctly recollected that there were *some* of them which were not disfigured at all. Now I could not account for this difference except by supposing that the roughened fragments were the only ones that had been *completely absorbed* – that the others had entered the whirl at so late a period of the tide, or, from some reason, had descended so slowly after entering, that they did not reach the bottom before the turn of the flood came, or of the ebb, as the case might be. I conceived it possible in either instance that they might thus be whirled up again to the level of the ocean, without undergoing the fate of those which had been drawn in more early or absorbed more rapidly. I made, also, three important observations. The first was, that as a general rule, the larger the bodies were, the more rapid their descent – the second, that, between two masses of equal extent, the one spherical and the other *of any other shape*, the superiority in speed of descent was with the sphere – the third, that, between two masses of equal size, the one cylindrical and the other of any other shape, the cylinder was absorbed the more slowly.

Since my escape, I have had several conversations on this subject with an old schoolmaster of the district; and it was from him that I learnt the use of the word "cylinder" and "sphere." He explained to me, although I have forgotten the explanation – how what I observed was, in fact, the natural consequence of the forms of the floating fragments – and showed me how it happened that a cylinder, swimming in a vortex, offered more resistance to its suction, and was drawn in with greater difficulty than an equally bulky body, of any form whatever.[1]

'There was one startling circumstance which went a great way in enforcing these observations, and rendering me anxious to turn them to account, and this was that, at every revolution, we passed something like a barrel, or else the yard or the mast of a vessel, while many of these things, which had been on our level when I first opened my eyes upon the wonders of the whirpool, were now high up above us, and seemed to have moved but little from their original station.

'I no longer hesitated what to do. I resolved to lash myself securely to the water-cask upon which I now held, to cut it loose from the counter, and to throw myself with it into the water. I attracted my brother's attention by signs, pointed to the floating barrels that came near us, and did everything in my power to make him understand what I was about to do. I thought at length that he comprehended my design, but, whether this was the case or not, he shook his head despairingly, and refused to move from his station by the ring-bolt. It was impossible to reach him; the emergency admitted of no delay; and so, with a bitter struggle, I resigned him to his fate, fastened myself to the cask by means of the lashings which secured it to the counter, and precipitated myself with it into the sea, without another moment's hesitation.

'The result was precisely what I had hoped it might be. As it is myself who now tells you this tale – as you see that I *did* escape – and as you are already in possession of the mode in which this escape was effected, and must therefore anticipate all

[1] See Archimedes *De Incidentibus in Fluido,* lib. 2.

that I have further to say – I will bring my story quickly to conclusion. It might have been an hour, or thereabout, after my quitting the smack, when, having descended to a vast distance beneath me, it made three or four wild gyrations in rapid succession, and, bearing my loved brother with it, plunged headlong, at once and for ever, into the chaos of foam below. The barrel to which I was attached sunk very little farther than half the distance between the bottom of the gulf and the spot at which I leaped overboard, before a great change took place in the character of the whirlpool. The slope of the sides of the vast funnel became momentarily less and less steep. The gyrations of the whirl grew, gradually, less and less violent. By degrees, the froth and the rainbow disappeared, and the bottom of the gulf seemed slowly to uprise. The sky was clear, the winds had gone down, and the full moon was setting radiantly in the west, when I found myself on the surface of the ocean, in full view of the shores of Lofoden, and above the spot where the pool of the Moskoe-ström *had been*. It was the hour of the slack – but the sea still heaved in mountainous waves from the effects of the hurricane. I was borne violently into the channel of the Ström, and in a few minutes, was hurried down the coast into the "grounds" of the fishermen. A boat picked me up – exhausted from fatigue – and (now that the danger was removed) speechless from the memory of its horror. Those who drew me on board were my old mates and daily companions – but they knew me no more than they would have known a traveller from the spirit-land. My hair, which had been raven-black the day before, was as white as you see it now. They say, too, that the whole expression of my countenance had changed. I told them my story – they did not believe it. I now tell it to *you* – and I can scarcely expect you to put more faith in it than did the merry fishermen of Lofoden.'

VII

The Day Trip

Patricia Daly

On Friday August the fifteenth nineteen-eighty Jane Despry, an actress with a touring theatre company, left the Severn Estuary by steamer bound for North Devon.

For some weeks the company had been in Bristol playing Shakespeare. Jane was not due to appear on stage until the following night for a performance of *The Tempest.* The decision to get away for the day had been taken on impulse. Her colleagues were busy rehearsing that evening's production, she found the little basement flat she had been given claustrophobic, and she was not in the mood for shopping or exploring the town. But she needed to perfect her lines and the prospect of a short voyage appealed to her.

'Do you mind awfully?' she had asked the producer, whose name was Andrew Paragon.

'Of course not.' He had looked at her with that slightly puzzled and indulgent expression which had become so familiar to her during the last year. 'We can spare you today. But don't get lost,' he had added. 'I'll wait up for you.'

She had been engaged to Andrew for three months, a handsome man of thirty, older than her by seven years, brilliant, sometimes moody. A man with an atmosphere at once dynamic and brooding, a loner. Orphaned as a child he had no family to speak of, while Jane was one of five. She was deeply in love with him but at times troubled by their relationship. An extrovert girl from a gregarious family she was not used to complex feelings. She was aware, even at this stage, there were certain things she could never share with Andrew.

*

In the wake of the pleasure steamer there rippled a ceaseless billow of foam. Jane leaned over the rail and stared at the deep green of the water. The sun and the wind, the cloudless sky calmed her restlessness.

The steamer had been the only one she had noticed on the dock that morning. A grizzled man in his fifties lolled in a chair on deck, presumably the captain. Above him was a sign: 'Day trips to glorious Devon and the Exmoor resorts. Only five pounds.'

Cheap enough she had thought. 'Is that return?' she had asked the captain.

'If you return, miss, you won't be charged more.'

She was wearing a navy two-piece with a white Peter Pan collar; her hair, a glistening cap of copper, was cut short in a fringe over her slanting hazel eyes. She had the soft clear skin of the red head. The captain smiled at her, showing crooked teeth in a face the colour of mahogany, and she paid her money into his big dry hand. The boat shuddered as it left the dock and the great rusty chain lay coiled, gleaming with water on deck. The crew were friendly but there seemed few passengers aboard.

Jane took out a slim moroccan-bound copy of *The Tempest* from her bag and opened it at the second scene. The Bristol Channel was smooth but the sun began to dazzle her eyes and she decided to go below for a while. The saloon which had an old musty smell of tobacco and spice, and something else she couldn't quite define, was almost deserted. Two men played cards and a woman sat in the corner a glass in her hand. The woman who had limp straw-coloured hair wore a pill box hat with a small veil and a black suit with padded shoulders. Her face was coarse-featured and heavily made up. When Jane looked again it seemed to her that the woman's eyes, pale blue and fishlike with drooping red lower rims, were swimming with tears.

A steward behind the bar dried glasses and she ordered a gin and lime. 'Been this way before?' he enquired and when she shook her head he asked her where she was bound for.

'A pretty little place,' he said when she told him. 'If you don't mind a climb.'

'Do you know it?' asked Jane.

'Oh yes, we often pass this way. But I'm stuck here like the rest.' He jerked his head in the woman's direction. 'Been hanging around for years. Ever since nineteen-thirty-eight.'

Jane smiled at the witticism. The woman was certainly dressed strangely. She was surprised, however, when the waiter refused her money. 'Have you time for another? We're nearly there.'

Jane refused gracefully and managed to slip a tip under the glass; then she hurried up on deck. They were approaching the shores of a bay. Beyond lay a small town at the foot of precipitous wooded hills. Two streams cascaded down deep combes to converge into an estuary which flowed into the bay. Along the street that fringed the stream were shops and cafés and on the shore a few thatched cottages and two hotels. As she watched, the scene seemed to waver as though in a heat haze and she blinked.

'It's low tide,' said one of the crew. 'We'll have to take you in by boat.' He beckoned a tall young sailor; a boat was lowered over the side and Jane was directed into it.

The sailor rowed, smiling now and again but saying nothing. The steady click of the oars against the rowlocks and the subdued hush of the waves tugging at the shingle were the only sounds that met her ears. But she suddenly felt chilled and drew her jacket closely around her.

'What time do you call back?' Jane asked as the boat ground on the pebbles near the tiny pier of the harbour. But the lad only smiled and Jane wondered if he spoke English. Somewhat flustered she embarked and clambered on to the quay. She looked for a notice giving the times of the boats but could not find one. Someone is bound to know, she told herself. But felt annoyed nevertheless.

Meanwhile the weather had changed. In a few moments, it seemed to her, the sky had turned livid and threatening and she found herself all at once in the middle of a steady downpour. The cliffs above were hidden in mist, their foliage dripping. Water hissed down over the rocks in a deep cleft to join the swollen, turbulent waters of the stream below. In the street people huddled in doorways. What a fiasco! she thought.

She sheltered for a while under the awning of a sweet shop and was amused to see old fashioned jars of boiled sweets in the window and faded carton replicas of Cadbury's Milk Tray. She went in and purchased a bag of mint humbugs. The girl behind the counter seemed annoyed when Jane proffered her a pound note. 'Haven't you anything smaller?' she said. Eventually she produced a number of shillings out of the till and Jenny shovelled the change into her handbag.

When she got outside it was to find that the rain had ceased as suddenly as it had begun. The sun shone: on the dripping trees, now visible, that clothed the slopes above; on the glistening shop fronts, some with panes of bottle glass; on the gushing stream where the water tumbled over boulders green with slime. From a clock above a drapery store she could see it was already twelve-thirty and she ascended the hill in search of a restaurant only to find them all full. The people inside looked at Jane curiously: at her smart navy two-piece, at her careful eye-make-up, at her short, layered hair.

She decided not to proceed and retraced her steps remembering one of the hotels on the harbour which looked inviting.

She had only just reached it when the skies opened once more and Jane hastened into the lobby. After studying the menu on the reception desk she went through into the dining-room, choosing a table near the window overlooking the harbour. Outside the scene was menacing: the sea far out, boiling with foam and a garish light on the shore. And then as she and the other diners watched they saw what seemed to be a gigantic movement in the sky. High above the horizon a great mass of fiery cloud moved slowly across while below it another mass, dark and purplish as a bruise, raced across the heavens in the opposite direction hiding the sun in a veil of darkness. There were exclamations of wonder. Round her the figures at the other tables looked shadowy in the gloom and someone put on the lights. A great flash of lightning illumined the bay.

A waitress came over to take her order. 'Dreadful weather,' Jane said conversationally.

'Oh we're used to it down here,' the girl said laconically. 'Won't come to nothing.' And Jane was reassured. The low murmur of the guests in the dining-room, the lashing of the rain at the window and the tumult outside all combined to induce in her a sense of safe and pleasurable solitude and once more she took out her copy of *The Tempest* and began going over her lines.

The place was beginning to fill up as people hurried in from the harbour and a couple looking for a table approached her. The man hesitated a moment as she met his eyes.

'May we join you?' he asked.

His face seemed so familiar that for a moment Jane found herself unable to speak. Then she realised her mistake, she had never set eyes on him before. And yet something nagged at her: a deep inexpressible recognition. 'Do,' she said.

He was young; still, she guessed, in his twenties; tall and lean with broad shoulders and dressed in a suit of Harris tweed. He had deep-set eyes of a brilliant blue and thick fair hair. Altogether, she thought, a very wholesome young man except for the eyes which were dreamy and sexually disturbing. The woman with him might have been slightly older, with dark and lustrous curly hair and thick-lashed brown eyes set in an oval face. She would have been a beauty but for the fact that her skin was sallow and her teeth stained with nicotine.

The waitress returned and, while the man ordered, the woman took a cigarette out of a silver case. 'Do you mind if I smoke?' she said. Jane shook her head: so many people in the room were smoking already it would have seemed illogical to object. The woman tapped the cigarette on the case and lit up. Her movements were nervous and highly charged and when she spoke it was in a low husky voice. She was, Jane decided, extraordinarily seductive although her skin was imperfect and her breath stale with tobacco smoke. While she and the man chatted she smiled at Jane now and again and two deep dimples appeared at the side of her mouth. The man made amused interjections; at one point over the fish course she reached across and took his hand in an utterly unselfconscious movement. It was obvious to Jane they were very much in love.

There was a sudden great peal of thunder and the windows rattled. 'What a day!' said the woman.

She told Jane that she and her husband were down on holiday and had left their two year old child with a nanny.

'We like this hotel,' she said. 'You see it has special associations.'

'Really?' Jane could not help liking this vivacious woman with her warm, effusive manner. The man looked at Jane with his dreamy pre-occupied expression. 'Very special,' he said.

It transpired that while she had been at university she had taken a job as a waitress. 'In this very hotel,' said the woman. 'I was hard up and needed the money. And the second day I was here Mark walked in.'

'Love at first sight,' Jane said smiling.

'More like second sight. We were both in our finals year and Mark was president of the dramatic society. Of which I was a humble member.'

'You were never humble, Rita,' he said. 'But you have imploring eyes.' He smiled at Jane. 'You should have seen her in the dining-room. Quite irresistible.'

Rita ate daintily with little appetite and smoked between courses. 'I love the way you do your hair,' she told Jane. 'Like a French fisher-boy's.' She leaned forward. 'Tell me all about yourself.'

*

Afterwards they went into the lounge for coffee. Rita had picked up Jane's copy of the Shakespeare. 'You'll make a perfect Miranda.' She read aloud from the text:

'If by your art, my dearest father, you have
Put the wild waters in this roar, allay them.
The sky, it seems, would pour down stinking pitch,
But that the sea, mounting to the welkin's cheek,
Dashes the fire out.'

She put down the book. 'Now that's a part I would have loved.'

'You play parlourmaids and waitresses best,' said Mark.

'Listen to him! And you, dear Miranda, for that is what I shall call you, are only down for the day. Can't you stay longer?'

'I have to get back tonight. I'm rehearsing early tomorrow,' said Jane.

Mark insisted on paying the bill and they accompanied her into the lobby. There had been another fierce cloudburst and the sky was a dark leaden hue except for the strange fiery streaks in the west. 'No boat is going to put out to sea in this,' Mark said. 'I'll drive you to Lynton. You can get a bus to Barnstaple from there and catch the train.'

The car was a fine old Buick, carefully tended and maintained except for the windscreen wiper which Mark manipulated by hand. Visibility was poor as they ascended the steep winding hill overhung by cliffs, where trees hung precariously, and great outcrops of rock which loomed suddenly out of the dimness. It was difficult to believe that it was still only three o'clock in the afternoon. Above the hiss of the rain was another more sinister sound, that of a torrent in full spate and now and again an ominous cracking.

'Goodbye, Miranda,' said Rita as they drew up at the bus station. 'We can't come any further than this. We have to stay in the storm.' She kissed Jane on the cheek.

'It'll be a long journey for you,' said Mark.

She looked back and in the wavering light saw for an instant Rita's pale face through the rear window of the car as she turned and waved. And it seemed to Jane that the face wore a beseeching expression before it was blotted out by the driving rain. It was the last she saw of them and she experienced a sudden sense of loneliness and desolation.

*

It was only while she was on the bus that Jane became aware of another strange phenomenon. The freakish weather had changed. Once again the skies had cleared and with an almost incredible rapidity. As the bus drove along at the side of the gorge she could see no sign of the recent storm. The little town far below shone peacefully in the sun, the stream in the centre a glittering silver thread.

Just my luck, she thought as she got rid of all the shillings in her bag on the driver. The journey to Barnstaple took over an hour and there was a long wait for a rail connection at Exeter. To add to her annoyance she found she had left behind her copy of *The Tempest*.

It was after ten when she finally arrived at the flat and she found Andrew waiting. 'I've been here since eight o'clock,' he said. 'I thought you'd be back long ago.'

He had taken some eggs out of the fridge in the alcove kitchen and began preparing an omelette. The flat itself was spacious and overlooked a whitewashed yard. Finding Andrew already there pleased Jane; his presence served to alleviate a piercing sense of loss that had persisted ever since she had said goodbye to Mark and Rita. 'You look as though you really belonged here,' she said.

'Well, what else? And where on earth have you been?'

'Lynmouth,' she said. 'I went by boat but had to return by train. The weather in the bay was terrible – there were fearful storms. Do you know the place?'

He shook his head. 'Only by hearsay. To tell you the truth I've never had any desire to visit that part of the world and I doubt that I ever will. What did you do?'

'I met a charming couple. We had lunch in the Beach Hotel and they drove me back to Lynton where I caught a bus to Barnstaple. It's been a hell of a journey.'

He finished cooking the omelette and turned it out on to a plate which he had warmed in the oven. 'The Beach Hotel,' he said. 'There's no Beach Hotel in Lynmouth; not any more. It was swept away in the flood disaster.'

'I remember reading about the flood,' said Jane. 'When the river burst its banks and engulfed the town. Funny, that's the first time I've thought of it today. But there is a Beach Hotel. I particularly remembered the name.'

Or had she? Looking back she couldn't be absolutely sure. But yes, she was sure.

'You're wrong,' he said. He took two wine glasses from a

pine sideboard and placed them on the table. 'I should know. My mother and father checked in at the Beach Hotel. On a Friday. They were both lost that night when the floods came. The fifteenth of August nineteen fifty-two. Nothing was left of the hotel.'

'I thought they died in a road accident,' she said.

He poured her a glass of wine and another for himself. 'Not strictly speaking. They were missing, presumed drowned. They must have been out when the water flooded the valley towards evening. The remains of the car were found some days later on the foreshore. The bodies were never recovered.'

'Poor Andrew,' she said.

'I was only two at the time. Staying at my grandmother's house in Oxford.'

There was a pause while Jane began on the omelette. 'Delicious,' she said. And a little later: 'What kind of car?'

'I've no idea. No, wait. I remember someone saying my father drove a Buick. Or was it a Packard? They were fond of the Beach Hotel. They met there apparently.'

'Not for the first time,' Jane said. 'She got a job as a waitress in the vacation. And he walked in. He was the president of the university dramatic society; they renewed acquaintance in the dining-room.'

Andrew smiled. 'You have a very fertile imagination,' he said. 'It could well have been something like that.'

'Your mother was very beautiful and alive. And a great talker. You have her eyes. But you take after your father.'

'Tell me more,' Andrew said with the indulgent, slightly puzzled expression she had grown to know so well.

'It was a strange sort of trip in the first place,' Jane continued. 'There was a woman on board who had been on the ship since nineteen thirty-eight.'

His eyes brightened. 'It gets better and better. Have some more wine.'

She felt vague, her mind blurring, her thoughts obliterated like a dream that slips away on waking as one tries to recapture it. She looked into the depths of Andrew's dark eyes and her head swam.

'Oh, Andrew!' she said.

He kissed her.

'We ought to talk about tomorrow's rehearsal,' she said. 'About Miranda. I have a new idea about her.'

'That can wait,' Andrew said.

*

She was getting breakfast next morning when there was a ring at the door. Andrew who had stayed the night was still in bed. They had never been so close, she thought. She was filled with an agreeable languor, an animal appreciation of the senses.

The postman stood at the front of the area steps a package in his hand. He was young and ginger-haired. 'Something to pay,' he said. 'Thirty pee.'

Jane took some silver out of her handbag and gave it to him but he made no move to depart. She opened the package. Inside a manilla envelope was the moroccan-bound copy of *The Tempest* with her name and address on the fly-leaf. A note slipped out.

> Miranda – we thought you might need this book which you left in the car. Hope this reaches you in time. Adieu. Rita and Mark Paragon.

The postman still hovered. 'Someone's having you on,' he said. 'The date's haywire.'

She looked at the postmark. Over an old sixpenny stamp it showed black and slightly smudged:

LYNTON –DEVON 4.30 pm 15 AUG 1952.'

She was still holding the envelope and the book in her hand when Andrew appeared.

'Anything in the post?' he asked.

'No,' she said. 'Nothing to speak of.'

She put the envelope and the note in the bin and made the coffee.

VIII

Poor Kate

Mary Williams

I saw Kate rushing, almost running, down the road to Pendillon station. I was surprised; I hadn't seen her for years – it must have been quite five – since the day she took off with some boyfriend or other only six months after her marriage to Robin Clee.

At the time the story had been the tasty talking point of our respectable residential suburbia. Robin, in the first place, had been a catch, and in the old term phraseology 'out of the top drawer', whereas Kate! well, she was no beauty. Smart and distinctive on occasion in her rather angular fashion but with no subtle charm of feminine glamour. She just hadn't an ounce of sex appeal, which made it more of a puzzle why Robin had fallen for her. Money probably, the uncharitable said. It was fact that in recent years the Clees had suffered heavily, financially speaking. And Kate was reasonably well off.

Still, the whole thing had been extremely odd, especially her desertion and with a man called Matt no one had ever heard of. Robin had seemed extremely cut-up; and everyone had thought he'd get a divorce but he hadn't – not at the time, anyway – although there was evidence enough, what with the letter and all the other tittle-tattle, concerning secret meetings in the woods, brief glimpses of her in some benighted road-house with a tall dark stranger, all the usual titillating scandal you read about in certain Sunday papers when lurid enough to hit the headlines. Kate's affair of course, hadn't been exactly head-line stuff. She'd just gone and not returned and that was that. Robin had left a couple of years later and taken off to Canada or New Zealand or somewhere. This was the last I'd heard; and really, until I saw Kate hurrying to the station on that certain early spring evening, I'd hardly given the matter any thought recently.

But the sight of her resurrected things in my mind with quite a jolt. There was no mistaking her tallish leggy figure, the way she strode along, head thrust a little forward, dark hair swinging back from one of those tricky pill-box little hats she went in for. Her coat, rather ostentatious and fur-trimmed at the hem, was swinging too. She was in some terrific hurry, I thought, and wondered why.

'Kate ... ' I called, hurrying after her, 'hey there ... Kate ... Kate ... ' thinking, 'why doesn't she stop? She can't be deaf?' And we'd known each other pretty well in the past when we'd worked in the same firm, Careys, Solicitors of Pendillon, taking the same journey back each evening to our respective homes, on the friendly slow-moving little train that had chugged then, so constantly along the branch-line leading from Halt to Halt.

On the last 'Kate' she turned, seemed to recognise me and paused briefly, enabling me to catch up with her. Twilight was already deepening into the soft lilac dusk, so reminiscent somehow of lost youth and half-forgotten dreams, taking the roof-tops, buildings and ghostly blossoming trees into muted half glimpsed shapes dotted intermittently with the glimmer of a light.

'Heavens!' I said, breathlessly. 'What's the hurry?'

Her face in the shadowed light, was no different, a little harder perhaps, older, but that was natural. '*You*,' she said. 'I wondered if ... oh, Jane, for pete's sake come on.' She started off again on her mad rush, like the White Queen or someone else in *Through the Looking Glass*. – 'It's six thirty already, and you know that damn train doesn't wait.'

'What train?' I managed to gasp, as we dashed on. 'There's no six thirty now ... you have to wait for the seven five ... '

'Of *course* there is. For heaven's sake! It'll be in now and there's so much to tell, it's been so long. We'll have a chance to talk at last ... '

Quite uncomprehending, knowing she was either playing

some stupid joke or had just arrived from the wilds somewhere and hadn't a clue how the old timetable had altered or been swept out altogether, I went along with her and as we pushed through the ticket office on to the platform, I saw, with amazement, that she was right. The little train was already waiting there, with the guard ready to wave his flag, blow his whistle or whatever he'd done in the past. I couldn't understand; it just didn't make sense. But Kate, apparently, had been in no doubt at all. Perhaps there was a trip or something, I thought, as I clambered into a carriage after her. Yes, that must be it – a special thing laid on for holiday makers.

But it was only March. The crowds didn't begin to come for weeks, months yet. Still, there must *be* an explanation. Kate would tell me. How ridiculous, that I hadn't heard myself.

When we'd both got our breath back, she threw me a sidelong glance and said a bit wistfully – at least, wistfully for Kate, she was usually rather forthright and matter-of-fact – 'What've I done, Jane? Why've you been avoiding me?'

'*Avoiding* you?' I echoed, astonished, to say the least of it. 'What a thing to say. You just haven't been around. Oh come on Kate, tell me about it.'

'About what?'

'Well ... ' I stared at her with a weird, shivering feeling creeping up my spine to scalp; She seemed so vague and remote somehow; so uncomprehending. And I wondered if she'd had a shock of some kind. She waited until I concluded, 'About your marriage, and why you did ... what you did ... '

'You mean fall for Robin?' She smiled at me with her lips, but not her eyes, although I couldn't be sure, what with the steam and curls of smoke billowing through the failing light as the train chugged on, stopping occasionally at the well-known small halts. 'Oh I don't know ... his looks, I suppose, charm. All the things he has a girl wants. We're going to be married next month you know. Or hadn't you heard?'

I didn't answer. She was obviously off her head or playing a trick. But Kate had never been one to do that sort of thing ...

Humour of the nice or nasty kind just wasn't in her character, which was why, I suppose, I'd found her frequently so boring.

'I see,' I said awkwardly, trying to match up to her mood, or game, or whatever it was she was playing at.

'We've got a gorgeous place at Roselynne,' she went on, in a half-dreamy, very *un*-Kate-ish voice, 'You must know it. The old Manor House, right off the main road ... '

Yes, I knew it. From the outside. But I'd never visited, simply because I'd never been asked. During the few months following the wedding I'd half expected an invitation and when it hadn't come had guessed the reason to be a social matter, never myself having moved within Robin's select orbit of friends. It hadn't worried me at all. Although we knew each other well, Kate and I had never been close; and anyway I hated cocktail parties, bridge, dinners and the usual gossipy gatherings of their special rich brand of humanity.

'I know it,' I answered automatically, 'Just by sight.'

'Well ... look ... ' she became suddenly uncharacteristically enthusiastic, almost vivacious. 'You must come along now ... next stop, remember? It's not far from there – five minutes, then you could hop back and catch the seven thirty to Fairfield.'

To say I was surprised is an understatement. I couldn't think straight any more; to hear her rambling on like that just as though it hadn't all happened years ago, as though she was about to step into matrimony with all the corny trappings about her of some young and beautiful bride, it really was too ridiculous. Or – a momentary feeling of unreality swept over me – a temporary fleeting aberration that made me doubt my own senses. Was it *me*? Or Kate? And why were we sitting in the steamy dusty carriage behind an engine that had surely gone to the scrap heap or wherever it was such things went, an age ago?

I glanced at her apprehensively. Her profile, staring into the thickened twilight, though subdued, was tangible and real. Strong nose, set jaw, straight dark hair, sophisticated unbecoming hat with a rosette on top of its upturned severe brim. Smart, as always. But unsubtle, without the first idea of how to make the best of herself. How on *earth*, I wondered for the hundredth time, had she managed to capture Robin Clee? *And* a lover into the bargain? And why was she here now? It was all wrong. *Kate* was wrong somehow, not me. Why should it be me, after a perfectly ordinary day at the office, with the prospect of an average evening ahead, television following a meal and then a hot bath and bed? The usual routine. The accepted way of life, since Tim's, my husband's death. At first it had been hard, almost too hard to bear, but in the end I'd got through, like so many woman did who had to face the same terrible situation – either win, or go under, land up in a mental home, or as an eccentric recluse.

Something clicked into place then. *Kate*. Perhaps she'd lost him, the mysterious lover who'd lured her from the security and comfort, a rich husband, all the things most girls long for ... into an unknown future possessing perhaps, nothing but her passion for him. And if he'd died, or thrown her up? 'Poor Kate,' I thought, with sudden swift sympathy, it must be that. He'd gone. She was alone and it was too much for her.

So when she urged me to go along with her, I couldn't, after the first doubts, refuse.

We both got out at Coldbrook and set off together from Roselynne.

'You must come for the evening sometime when we're really settled in,' Kate suggested dreamily, as we climbed the thread of lane winding through bushes and trees towards a crossroads, where one track cut back again towards the house.

'Don't be a chump, Kate,' I said sharply, rattled and on edge by her 'off-beat' absurd, remark. '*When* you're married. Go on; stop it. It's potty carrying on like that.'

'*Why?*' She really *did* sound dumbfounded and my spine chilled again, as I wondered if she really *had* gone out of her mind.

'I don't see anything potty about getting married,' she persisted, adding pointedly, 'What's the matter with you, Jane? Jealous?'

Jealous? Oh my God! I thought. If only she had a clue what she was doing to me. *Jealous*? Of Robin Clee? When I'd had *Tim* and as near-perfect a marriage as there could be on earth? Pain cut through my anger, stifling the hot reply on my lips. I walked on silently refusing to be goaded and after a moment

Kate mumbled something like, 'No. I suppose not. I shouldn't have said that. Forget it.'

Near the top of the hill we took the turn to Roselynne. The trees had thinned there, becoming a mere tracery against the deepening violet sky, lit at intervals by the glimmer of early blossom from the hedges. The air was fresh; laden with the faint almost intangible drift of flowers, violets, primroses and mingled scents of thrusting spring undergrowth. The following week, it would be April and I recalled, with renewed poignancy T.S.Eliot's poem 'Burial of the Dead' beginning 'April is the cruellest month, breeding lilacs out of the dead land.'

'Oh, Tim, Tim,' I thought, 'why did it have to happen? Why did you have to leave me?' I did not usually indulge in self pity any more. Experience had taught me the futility of too much looking back. For survival one had to go ahead. But this walk with Kate, somehow had already flung me into the past again, resurrecting emotions I'd thought were dead, or at least extinguished sufficiently not to hurt. Ironic, I thought, I should have had to meet her after so long, on an evening like this, pre-ordained by nature to open old wounds by its enchanted lush quality of youth and longing and unexplainable, almost unendurable sweetness.

I must have quickened my pace involuntarily, because she broke through my thoughts by saying, 'Steady on. No need to run. We're almost there. Look!'

Through the pale grey of silver birch and pines, I saw across an approach of long grass, starred by the frail evening-dimmed gold of daffodils and jonquils, the grey façade of the early Georgian mansion I'd seen once or twice but never until now visited.

'This is the front,' Kate announced. 'But the best part with the terraces and gardens is at the back. Sorry the drive's so overgrown here. But in a way it's rather nice, don't you think? Picturesque? Sort of ghostly.'

Her words, the manner in which she spoke chilled me. I wished I'd never made the jaunt with her at all. In the first place, I should certainly not be back at Coldbrook in time to catch my usual train; in the second, well, everything was becoming just too incomprehensible and weird.

'Look here ... ' I burst out and the sound of my own voice was comforting in the dead silence of the garden, 'I *must* hurry, Kate. I've got to get back. There's the dog to let out. Mrs Clarke left at three. Besides I'm hungry ... '

Kate appeared not to hear. *She* was in a hurry now, striding ahead of me so that her leggy figure at times was completely lost in the shadows of trunks and looming building where, whatever strange idea had got into her head, she had once lived with Robin.

As she inserted her key into a side door, the explanation occurred to me suddenly that she might be returning, that she *was* getting married, for a *second* time and that her reference to 'Robin' had merely been a slip of the tongue, or perhaps I'd misheard and the name had been Robert. Yes. That could so easily be the case and one that I was grateful to accept, forgetting the series of other small incidental remarks that just didn't make sense.

'Of course,' she said, as she switched on the hall lights, 'it's been neglected for such a long time. People have been coming and then leaving again for ages. Such a pity and yet lucky for us. Still there'll only be the cleaning to do and a bit of decorating perhaps. Everything's intact, furniture, fitments, all just waiting.Come on, I'll show you the front rooms first.'

I followed her down the wide hall to rooms on opposite sides, immediately before a spiralling wide staircase led off on the right hand, overlooked by a blue and gold stained-glass window.

The atmosphere was cold and deserted, completely silent except for the hollow echo of footsteps as we trod the mosaic floor. Mine were loud, uncomfortably so; whereas Kate's ... but then she was obviously wearing some type of foam-rubbered things that had no impact at all.

'There,' she said, throwing the drawing room door wide, and switching the lights full on. 'Isn't it quite sumptuous in an old world way?'

I stared at the brocade upholstered furniture and hangings so dust-laden that their colour, a muted shade of pink, was mostly no more than powdered grey, at the hanging crystal lustres and chandeliers, their primal glory dimmed by cob-webs dropping from the ornate ceiling, casting their shroud over walls and dadoed skirtingboard, across the floor.

A dead room. Lost. A room for those gone rather than the living.

'Well?' Kate persisted in anxious tones, as though my opinion, ridiculously, was of utmost importance.

'Yes,' I agreed, with constraint. 'Yes … it *could* be, with a bit of cleaning up.'

'Oh *that*,' she sounded annoyed then. 'Well, naturally, after so long. I said so, didn't I? What did you expect? The dining room's the same I guess. But basically it's got great dignity. And don't say it hasn't, Jane. And for God's sake keep your prim little thoughts to yourself about wanting tidying up and all that.'

I did.

I let her lead me from room to room, down wide passages, through a maze of smaller corridors, cloak rooms, kitchens, pantries, upstairs through majestic bedrooms, all bearing the same indefinable atmosphere of neglect and decay, weighted with an overall sense of depression that tempted me to make a dash for the door and escape. Escape from what? Kate? But how stupid really, I told myself, with an effort to squash an inner rising panic. Kate was Kate. Just a woman I'd known and once worked with as a girl. Or was she?

As she passed under a light, saying, 'I'll show you the garden now …' I saw for the first time how really pale she was, how large and hungry looking her brown eyes were under their thick brows. And the trembling of her thin fingers, with their enlarged knuckles as they caressed, lovingly, each shelf, curtain, corner of chair or table … they were no longer the prosaic strong hands of Kate Pettigale who had typed so efficiently on the office typewriter. They were almost luminous; greedy though, in a way unpleasant, but pitiful too.

So I controlled myself sufficiently to follow her through the nearest door, down half a dozen steps into a drive which led directly to a garden at the back of the house. The light was now so dim, nothing was really visible but a mere indication of darker shapes against the velvet grey of evening, criss-crossed in patches by the phantom glimmer of paths under dense shrubs and trees, and the faint glassy sheen of a pool shrouded by drooping foliage.

'Look, Kate ... ' I began. 'I'm sure it's attractive, but let me come back another time. It's silly trying to see anything properly now. Besides I nearly lost my shoe just there; a stone or something ... '

'No. It isn't far,' she urged, almost whispering. 'It's important ... ' She glanced back, touching my hand lightly. I shivered; her own was so cold, as though all life-blood had been drained away. I was suddenly terrified, filled with a sick kind of fear intensified by her own urgency, the sense of isolation and brooding quietness, which now enfolded us into a strange hinterland of unreality, of territory uncharted by humanity.

And yet I couldn't break away. Something stronger than my own will, forced me to follow her, as she cut to one side abruptly, across the soft thick grass, starred by the pale ghost-faces of spring flowers. Then, quite suddenly she stopped. A little wind shivered across the earth, brushing our forms lightly, as she lifted one arm saying. 'There it is ... the apple tree.'

I stared at the pale blossoming tree ahead, which in the morning, I knew, would be a foam of pearly-white against the sky. Now like the rest of the terrain, it was a ghost tree, lit with a luminous unearthly beauty, holding in that highly-charged moment of awareness however, menace and intense foreboding of evil.

I tried to move, but Kate's hand clutched my wrist.

'There it is,' she said, pointing to a patch of ground immediately beneath the tree. 'That's it.'

'What?' I whispered, half apprehending the answer.

'My grave,' she said simply. 'Where Robin laid me. He put me there, one night in the fog, and I've been waiting ever since, watching for you ... on the six thirty ... but you were never there, somehow, at the right time. He was a devil, Jane. Greedy; but not for me ... just ... what I'd got ... '

I waited horrified, frozen, until her voice, wan now, already fading continued, 'That's why no one's stayed here. I didn't want to scare them, but just sometimes I had to be around.

Now it will be all right. The council's bought it. Did you know? And tomorrow they'll be starting digging to build flats or something … ' The faint wail died for a moment into the echo of trembling laughter, which could have been merely the wind's shuddering sigh.

'Kate … ' I managed to call. 'Kate … ' but she was no longer there; and there was no sound any more except perhaps, words from very far away, which might have been I suppose, just a trick of imagination. 'It's been hard … wandering about in two times … '

Then, quite suddenly, everything changed.

I was alone, on the road to Pendillon station, with the twilight falling, folding the hedgerows and distant roofs of the town into grey uniformity.

There was the rattle of a train from the distance. I must have been standing there for – how long? There was no knowing; and I didn't, just then, bother to try; just started running and ran and ran, until I reached the platform in the nick of time to catch the usual seven five for home.

*

During the following week I tried, in leisure moments to put the weird episode from my mind, telling myself, though hardly convincingly, that I'd imagined it all, suffered from some unknown reason, a hallucination, resurrected possibly from a nightmare, by a chance word, phrase, or combination of circumstances at the office that day. Freud or Jung would have come up with an explanation; but as I was no specialist in psychology, I shut it from my thoughts – at least *consciously*; deciding that if there was a recurrence, I would see a doctor.

Nothing happened though. Kate did not re-appear, neither did the elusive six-thirty train. In fact I learned there'd been *no* train at that time, not even a special trip in the 'season' since it had been taken off those years ago.

I was beginning to regard the whole affair in a comparatively light manner, when something *did* arise which gave me a shock.

Roselynne was taken over by the council, as my phantom

Kate had predicted, though at a later date than was expected, owing to some belated enquiries concerning conservation.

Anyway, it was July before the plan for erecting flats was properly started and workmen got busy clearing the land, for sewerage, drainage and the necessary essentials entailed for a modern building site.

Much of the timber was cut down and carted away, including an ancient apple tree that was already in a state of half decay.

It was during this operation that the body of a woman was found buried there, unidentifiable except for the teeth and a curious pewter bangle on the skeleton wrist bearing the initials K.C. engraved in an ornate monogram on its inner side.

Robin had been very careless there, I thought musingly.

Poor Kate.

But then perhaps it was 'poor Robin' too; because he was located not long afterwards, living contentedly and in apparent luxury with his new young blonde wife in the South of France, on the ample fortune so conveniently provided by his 'first'.

I have often wondered since the flats went up, whether the new occupants have been disturbed by any sinister illusion, or unexpected footsteps where they should not be.

Nothing, so far, has come to my ears; no notice either, in the press.

But one thing is sure; I would not live there for 'all the tea in China' in the words of the old adage.

As I said ... poor Kate. A terrible end; but then if she'd not been such a deadly bore of a woman, perhaps none of it would have happened.

IX

The Coastguard

Lanyon Jones

I remember the wild marshes; far horizon like a curlew call, the sky a moving panoply of shadow, high, bright air. A lone child among the dykes and sea shore, the reflected still waters of the narrow dyke, the white capped spray of the pebbled crunching ridge. Wind-bent thorns along winding empty lanes, flat, harsh, green, yellow, and always the massive moving legions of the upper air; free wind and salt heavy breach running damp on the macs and window panes.

No gull's cry, but the distant call of wild fowl – empty and longing across deserted tufts and saltings.

The deep dark blackness of the night, with specks of golden yellow mapping out man's habitation, and the sound of the groaning waves dragging out our pebble defences along the coastguard cottages.

I remember the lamps in the evenings, the cold tumble through the door, the slash of pelting dampness and 'foul night' murmurs from the shuffling adults as they bent over beer on the trestle. Salt spray on licked lips and cold hands moistened by the clinging wetness of thick woollen jumpers.

And the word that Harry would be abroad, as watery eye surveyed the blustering gloom against the window. The old rose – thorn dancing in the wind, illuminated by the oil-lamp – set to show him the way home; if ever he came.

Grandpa in shining black oilskins and jumper looking round and pointing a calloused bony finger.

'The lad.'

And the muttering of the first who spoke, and calling for more beer through their pipe smoke. Whilst the wind would rise and the slattering of rain would force a silence on the bulky steaming figures in the lamplight.

And the lone boy would sit – against the settle on the broad clean flags watching the changing pattern of wet boot marks on the stone. A halfpenny across the board and interest diverted from silent thoughts of old Harry out in the blustering cold, where he deserved to be.

The banging of a shutter, and the high call of a wind beaten bird crying overhead? But they were used to that, and the boy was not supposed to know. But old Anna would say, for she remembered the past, more now than her misty half-white eyes could comprehend today.

'It was on a night like this – and the signal fired, out there.'

But a horny hand would demand more ale and she would amble away, muttering her story into the back cellar. And the shutter would bang and a man would look about him through the blue coils of rising smoke, but not a word was said – the storm would blow itself into the marshes by morning.

And I remember the wetness of the wind on the face, the sound of Grandpa's pipe hissing, and looking down at the striding seaboots and muddy gullied lane. The roaring of the tide sweeping up and groaning down and flecks of weed and salt whipping across the ridge. And thinking of the dead men climbing out but dragged back to their cruel green graves by the groaning surging rush.

And Grandpa's bony hand as if he knew the thoughts – or feared for his charge when Harry may lurk wet and sunken-eyed behind the bastions of the little church. And the howl of something passing, brought up by the sea wind, and the swinging lamps and splash of those shapes trudging home. Gruff farewells and little comment of him who lay below the wiry tufts of the stone-hemmed, windswept churchyard.

The salt and screaming cold was good though, then, and I can remember it clear when the sea sings in a lonely place; like the white dry rumple of sheets and the cold feel without the stone bottle. And the wind would rattle at the window pane and the smell of lamp and sound of adult speech would seem far further than the curved stair actually was.

But there the boy would lie, half afraid lest he see, half that he would miss that wet misery of the face pressed against the teeming pane. The beard ahung with weed, dripping of salt damp as when they had dragged it white and stiffening from its chosen retribution, where the tide grinds the pebble ridge.

It was his due, that man, and, heart quickening and eyes straining in the dark room, cold toes wriggled in the tight confines of the safe cocoon, the boy would wait, but anticipation waned with the smell of clean linen and the growing warmth of a snug bed, it makes a boy drowsy which drifts into sleep. And there, in slumber the boy can remember, and pity the man. But it was his due, that nagivator, too drunk to do his charge, and the others, still rolling among the shifting darkness of green graves, do they remember the navigator? On windy stormy nights like this it is them that he remembers, he remembers his duty, but too late. It is the sign when he remembers the foundering ship, the fatal signal sent into the driving squally night. They knew their duty, but do they remember as he does, when he comes knocking?

The biographer put the papers down for a second time. Peculiar, the things one finds. It's certainly not his usual style.

He looked around the office, against one corner were stacked the famous Jeffries' *History of the Napoleonic Wars.* He picked up a green bound book from the desk; *Tank battles of the 1939-45 War* by D.R. Jeffries. The biographer grunted. Not his style at all – bit fanciful. He scanned the loose papers that had fallen from a file. Nothing else in the file except old photographs and, extraordinarily enough, three pebbles. He looked at the photographs. They were very old and a little torn. Must have been him as a child. Funny he should keep these in a file. The biographer idly placed the papers back in the file with the photographs. 'Can't see the point in this one,' he said to himself. He stared at a photograph of the interior of a room. It looked like a bedroom, it was night or else there was a shade against the window. An old iron bedstead just in the picture. A badly exposed photograph anyway. He sniffed and placed all the papers together and closed the file.

'I really must get on.' He pushed the file away and began to scan his notes on the early life of D.R. Jeffries.

'Well, that will have to do.' He felt irritated by the shortness of time he had in which to produce his monthly 'Insight Into.' If only the editor had given him more time – though of course, Jack could hardly know that old Jeffries was going to die like that. Nevertheless, ten days were hardly enough to get to grips with the real inside character of anyone – let alone Brigadier General Sir Desmond Jeffries. It was at this inconclusive point that the door opened – 'Want some tea, sir?'

The biographer was a little cheered. 'Thanks a lot, I could just do with a cup. Is Lady Jeffries still in?'

'No, she has gone out for a time, but gave instructions for you to be given tea at four.'

Thoughtful old dear, she had had quite enough to deal with during the last few months, and now letting him do the article on her husband, good old stick. He stirred his tea vigorously and attended to the important decision of which biscuit he would have first.

Maybe Lady Jeffries could throw some light on this file ... he would have to ask her sometime.

It was past six when the biographer packed his things together and left the office. Lady Jeffries was still not in when he enquired, so he went out of the house, descending the stone steps to the gravel driveway. It was a beautiful summer evening and he followed his inclination to walk rather than ride home through the West London suburb. It was a pleasant, quiet evening.

In strict contrast he sat awake in a cold sweat at 4.00 a.m. – he could not imagine what had given him such a terrible night.

A strange, recurring dream had dominated his restless hours. It opened with a bedroom, it seemed familiar, but as he thought about it he couldn't remember when he had been in the room. The dream continued with wind howling, and he felt a curious, anticipatory excitement mixed with a feeling of fear. He would look up from time to time at the window with a growing, prickling dread. The dream seemed always to end there, he would wake, cold sweat standing on his neck and forehead – then in half-consciousness he felt he heard a banging on the window, but now fully awake, he was not so sure. He lay awake in the light of his bedside lamp, he would have gone to get a book, but felt disinclined to traverse the dark landing beyond his bedroom door.

At five or six when daylight began to brighten his room he must have finally slept, for he awoke later to the jangle of his alarm clock.

It was not until he got to the house in the west London suburbs that he actually spoke to anyone. The young maid's face expressed a little concern when he arrived.

'Have you not had a good night, sir?' was her greeting.

He caught sight of himself in the hall mirror, and certainly had to admit he looked a little haggard.

But he began his work manfully and was soon absorbed in unravelling some of the personal details of Jeffries' younger days at Oxford.

It seemed that as a young man, Jeffries had taken quite an active part in a society known as 'The Friends of the Unhappy Departed' – a very strange sort of occupation for one who was to become so involved with such terrestrial activities as warfare. The biographer made little note of this youthful pastime – hardly the sort of mainstream characteristic of which the reading public would be grateful. One had to be so careful when handling heroes of the British past, careful not so much to hide unsavoury or unusual characteristics, but to be sure that the more unusual things were part of the man's total view of life. Obviously this little cult was by way of a youthful digression into the lunatic fringe, hardly worth a mention compared with the rest of his life! It was apparent that Jeffries soon lost interest in this, and, the biographer noted with gratitude, seemed to plant his feet on the road towards an Army career.

It was about mid-morning that Lady Jeffries came in to see how the work progressed. She was indeed a kind lady and was concerned to hear of the biographer's unpleasant night, he told her of the strange sensation and the dream. She listened with interest and was thoughtful:

'Desmond used to have similar bad nights. He would get up and do some writing. He had always wanted to write a particular book – he started it as a boy, but didn't bother with it much. As far as I know he only worked on it when he really couldn't sleep.' She looked thoughtful. 'I'm afraid it never really got very far ... strange really, he was so prolific in other directions.'

The elderly lady gazed around her husband's old work room. She had grey eyes which almost matched her hair. The biographer thought what a fine woman she must have been in earlier years.

'Oh, whilst you're here, Lady Jeffries.' The biographer went to the desk, and, sorting through a pile of papers, came upon the file. 'Do you know what this is?' He held it up.

'Why, yes.' She came towards him, taking the file from his hands, 'It's odd you should ask,' she opened it and turned over some of the papers it held. 'These are the notes Desmond made for the book I mentioned. I've never seen the inside of the file, but I have seen him with it when he couldn't sleep. He would perhaps use it two or three times a year, but it was good for him to have something there – it calmed him down.'

She looked through some of the notes.

'Have you read any of it?'

'Only a little, I found it yesterday. May I take it this evening, I can perhaps get something from it.'

'Why, of course – you may use any material you find here – old soldiers have few secrets, I'm afraid.' She smiled at him and handed the file back.

'Well, I really must be going, I hope all goes well with your work; and if I don't see you before this evening, do have a better night.'

After finishing for the day, without seeing Lady Jeffries again, he returned to his lodging. He took the file with him. He was tired after his day's work, and, although intending to look into the file before turning out his light, a drowsiness came over him, and he left the file unopened on a little table near the door.

It was about 3 a.m., after much tossing and turning, that he came to semi-consciousness. The sound of high winds penetrated his slumbering mind and the window rattled into his consciousness. He could not afterwards be sure, but the room seemed far darker than usual, as if the street lighting had been turned off. He had again the strong impression of his dream the previous night, that the room in which he slept was somehow different, that feeling of a certain dread came back to him. Again and again he tried to move his gaze from the darkened window, but his vision seemed to be dragged unwillingly, unerringly, back to the black space in the wall. He could hear a groaning noise outside, hard to distinguish, until he recognised it as the sound of the sea, – a tempest was rising. He awoke suddenly. Sitting up in bed he had a hot oppressed feeling, his palms and his face were damp with perspiration. He stared about himself in the darkness, trying to wake fully, but he could still hear the sounds of the sea and wind echoing in his mind. His throat was dry, and he shook his head trying to rid himself of the noises that seemed to have entered his head.

But they wouldn't go, he was sure he could hear them, he must still be asleep. He stumbled from the bed to the window, the sounds of the gale were still plain. He pulled the sash window up and leaned out to get fresh air. It was quiet and still in the street outside, and an electric street lamp shone encouragingly. He withdrew his head. But there again came the oppressive feeling, the sea groaning and crashing. He blinked into the dark room, he looked around, where were the sounds coming from? A gull cried as it was swept overhead by the howling wind. He stumbled across the room. Someone was playing a foolish game on him. He threw his clothes to the floor in the darkness and overturned a chair. His mind raced to find an answer.

It must be a tape recorder hidden somewhere in his room, he got closer to the door, the sounds seemed louder. There was the table with the file.

The noises seemed to be coming from the file, the noises were getting louder as he closed on the table by the door, another sound invaded his mind, a tapping, a tapping on his bedroom window. Someone was outside trying to get in. He grabbed up the file and turned on the light.

Everything was still, in the room. The net curtains moved a fraction in a light breeze where he had left the window open. His clothes and overturned chair were in a heap in the middle of the floor. He sank down on a chair by the door, holding the file to his chest. What a terrible dream! It had been worse than the night before, following him even as he walked. Thank goodness for the electric light!

He got back into bed and left the light on. Although he took the file to bed with him he somehow could not bring himself to look inside. He sat most of the night, but finally slept. He awoke the next morning to find the light still burning, and the file still held to his chest. He had a stiff neck, and certainly did not feel like work!

It was later that morning that the biographer actually reopened the file he had taken home the night before. The notes and photographs lay on the desk with the four pebbles, they all looked strangely pedestrian in the daylight. The shock came when he looked through the photographs, he recognised the photograph of the bedroom, it was the very same as his dream. He sat staring at the photograph and assured himself that there must be a logical answer. The fact that dreams are inspired by things one has seen in the day was the answer. They were used to work out one's problems. He knew the theories of dreams well enough, but could not see the significance of this one. He idly handled the four rounded pebbles. A frown wavered between his eyebrows and he looked into his right hand ...

Surely there had been three? He looked at them more closely. Just four small round stones, worn round by the surge of the sea, he surmised. Why had he thought there were only three, he must have been mistaken, it's hardly the sort of thing that really mattered anyway.

He put them down and picked up the sheaf of papers from the file. He had read the first couple of sheets already. Yes, those were the ones with the odd style, he looked through the sheets attached. It all seemed to be in this different style, disjointed jottings of a page or more at a time. He glanced from sheet to sheet trying to glean a connecting thread. He made a few notes.

The earlier parts – he presumed them earlier purely by the

childlike hand and aged quality of paper, and handwriting itself – as far as the style went could all have been written within days of one another. The earlier pieces made mention of a visitor, they all seemed concerned with the sea, the night, stormy weather. There was mention of a grandfather – the biographer presumed this to be Jeffries' own grandfather. More mention of a visitor, the visitor seemed to be purely nocturnal, the biographer grunted as he read on.

Odd bits seem to be conversations, or rather half a conversation, like an overheard telephone conversation. These were peculiar. There was mention of a promise, more recent pages seemed to indicate the promise not fulfilled, the other party getting angry and demanding, seemingly with some kind of menace, but there was nowhere a record of what the other party actually said. The most recent pieces were written in a less legible hand, it was obvious that Jeffries' illness was affecting even this part of his private life. His pen dug deeply into the paper as he seemed to protest that he had tried to fulfil some obligation. The biographer presumed this was the earlier promise made in childhood. Jeffries seemed to become quite frantic, though as the biographer surmized it could well have been the rapid decline into insanity that brought about the change in the writing.

The style did change towards the end, from a logical sequence into a rambling commentary of his early life, scattered throughout were references to his attempts to do justice to the book and more and more loomed the figure of Old Harry.

The biographer began to realise the connection that lay between the man Harry and the unnamed visitor. He came to the end and sat back in his desk chair. He had an uneasy feeling, a bubbling excitement, almost an anticipation, but couldn't quite put it into words, not even to himself. He again handled the pebbles and wondered if there had actually been just three before – if there had then why had another been put with them, by whom had it been put there. His thoughts raced on: 'The pebble-crunching ridge'; this story may bring him far more than his usual cheque for freelance articles. He had had the file with him since the last time he had looked. And most of all – where did the extra stone come from? He looked at them again, they had been worn round by the continuous action of the sea. He wondered, he took up the papers again and prepared to make a closer study.

It was some time later that day that the biographer encountered Lady Jeffries, and lost more time from his original work in taking his new inquiry a step further. It was from she that he extracted that Jeffries had indeed spent part of his childhood with his grandfather in a lonely village on the flat south coast marshes.

The biographer spent a good part of that afternoon in pursuit of something which Lady Jeffries could only deduce as frivolous. He, however, seemed to grow in excitement and interest. He was at pains to discover exact dates and place names of this early period in her husband's life. Lady Jeffries assured him that the village of Worsey had been of little importance in her husband's life. He hadn't visited it since childhood, and had in fact seemed disinclined to return there.

The biographer however, seemed of a different view, and that night, borrowed maps, notes and the mysterious file. He left the Jeffries' household and excused himself from work the next day.

That night was another spent wakefully by the biographer – but he was wakeful with some purpose. He waited, in the darkness armed with both notebook and tape recorder by his bed. All was quiet until two-thirty, he had dozed fitfully, wondering if he had been correct in his extraordinary conclusions of the afternoon. As he waited the afternoon seemed far distant and small. But then, as he moved restlessly, he had a growing awareness of something in the room, at first it was indistinct and unclassified, but it grew, little by little.

He turned to the tape recorder and pushed the button, the spool came to life, and pulled the tape through the recorder. He waited, his hand lying across his camera.

At first only the indistinct rustling of paper invaded his senses, the direction was difficult to gauge, but he felt sure it came from the area where earlier that evening, he had left the file.

It was some moments before he realised the wind was

beginning to rise, his attention was distracted from searching the gloom by the cry of a gull, seemingly high above, the sounds of the sea grew, little by little until he could have been certain that a gale was blowing outside. The sea surged and groaned – as if dragging back along a stony beach. The air felt hot within the bedroom, he had forgotten to open the windows that evening. He wondered if he would disturb the phenomenon he was witnessing if he got out of bed to open the window. It hadn't the night before, so he slid quietly from his bed.

As he crossed to the curtains a feeling of oppressiveness assailed his senses. It was ridiculous of course, as he was quite awake and was in no danger, merely plotting the course of this strange phenomenon, but he felt almost impelled to keep back from the window. He resisted the impulse.

As he drew back the curtains he seemed to see a reflection, far back, of something behind him in the room. It moved a little, and he turned to see what it was. Nothing stirred in the room; he noticed with surprise that the sounds had stopped, and a hush fell upon the room, almost as if it were holding its breath.

The biographer felt uneasy, this was not what he had anticipated. He again looked into the window, and there, in the far distance, he saw something somewhat denser than its surroundings. It moved again, and seemed to draw nearer. He had the notion that this was not a window at all, but in fact a mirror, it had a strange grey sheen, and he suddenly realised that he couldn't see the electric street light that stood below his lodgings.

He looked deep into the window, but could see only two small lamps burning, far away it seemed. They must have been held by someone, for they moved from one side to the other drawing closer, then back, from one side to the other. It was an odd feeling but the biographer became aware that the lamps were not far below, as one would expect if they had been at street level, but seemed to be on a level with himself.

He had enough of this, and drew away from the window. He would turn the light on and read for a time. He went towards where he knew the door to be. 'Drat!', he stubbed his foot against a large piece of furniture. He felt it, a chest of drawers? He hadn't got a large chest of drawers in his room, he quickly made for the light switch, but it wasn't there. He fumbled with the wall, he must have lost his sense of direction, he was sure he had come to the door. He made his way around the wall – he came to a fireplace, but he hadn't got a fireplace. He felt along the top, a candle holder, his fingers moved along the top. Wet wax, the candle had only just been extinguished. Where the hell was he?

A tapping distracted him. He looked round. It was a tapping on glass; his eyes strained to see the window. He could make it out as a lighter patch in the darkness, his heart pounded, was someone trying to get in? Into where? He didn't know where he was. The sounds of the tempest crashed upon him again, and the window was splattered with slattering rain. And then, he began to see something move outside the window, a denseness in the blustering gloom; it moved nearer, and then the face, wet and dripping, pressed itself against the streaming pane, white and ghastly the face pressed itself against the window – the eyes were open – but did not see him – they were glassy, fish-like eyes, the eyes of a long dead man.

It was nine o'clock when the biographer awoke. He had a headache, the bedroom was too stuffy and hot. He went to open the window, he stood looking down at the suburban street below, a phrase had come into his mind, unbidden;

'Can I come in?' it said. 'Can I come in?' He grunted; a peculiar thing to think. It had no significance until he came back to the bed, the tape recorder hummed, he had left it on the night before. The memory of his night came back to him with clearness, the clearness of reality he felt; he shivered.

There would be nothing on the tape of course, but he played it back to himself, just in case, but predictably; nothing. He went out to wash, and it was then that he noticed something on his left index finger – it was hard, like set glue; he put his thumb-nail under it and it chipped off and fell into the sink. It was wax – white candle wax. The biographer returned to his room and opened the file – he counted the pebbles that lay at the bottom.

It was of considerable surprise to both Lady Jeffries and his editor when the biographer informed them that he was taking a short vacation. He assured his editor that his monthly 'Insight Into' would be ready and that next month he would write the promised article on Sir Desmond Jeffries, but this month the editor would have to wait and see.

The *Monthly Review,* he was informed, could not be expected to wait for one contributor to get around to producing his own thing in his own fashion, but the biographer was unswayed in his determination to take some time at the coast. The editor could hardly argue with a contributor of his abilities. The biographer could well go elsewhere, and probably be paid more too, so the editor capitulated.

So it was that the biographer took a train that afternoon for the coast. The journey was a long one from London and he had time to take a good look through the extraordinary file he had been carrying. He sifted through the papers with a disconcerting awareness that he actually expected to find something new. Putting his hand into the bottom of the file he felt something damp against his fingers, and withdrew the pebbles, six rounded pebbles. One seemed damp; he looked at it more closely, and held it up. Just a pebble worn round by the sea, almost as if he had just picked it up from a beach – but it soon dried in the warmth of the railway compartment. There was no need he thought, the fifth had done its work. He had got the message. He smiled; he was taking up the invitation.

The photographs lay on his lap. The photograph of an interior was a room he recognised – the photograph from D.R. Jeffries' childhood struck him forcibly. It was of a window, a grey mist outside and near the window, by the wall, a large old chest of drawers, he remembered that; he had hit his foot on it.

It was drawing towards dinner time when the biographer arrived at the small local station of his destination. Worsey Halt consisted of two narrow raised platforms lifted above the surrounding water meadow. Reeds grew up and out of the marsh about the far end of the platform, and the station-master's house seemed to grow like a pale yellow fungus, at the other end. The two railway tracks petered out into the dusk in either direction. The dominating view of this damp low lying place seemed to be the sky, there was more of it than anything else. Away to the south stretched the long high ridge of stones that formed the pebble bank, the sea-defence of this salt marsh dotted with cottages and farms. The biographer looked at his luggage and then around. He spied a figure with cap and boots that stood in the shadows by the corrugated tin waiting room, obviously a porter hoping his services would not be required. 'I say, could you help me with the bags?' The figure did not move. The biographer called again across the platform. 'Excuse me, could you give me a hand … ' The figure moved a little, stepping back into the shadows.

'Not much of a welcome,' the biographer muttered to himself. He picked up his case and bag, trying to balance his typewriter and briefcase.

He had walked down the platform a short way when a door opened in the station-master's house, a light shone out of the door into the quiet dusk, the yellow light made the day look darker than he had thought.

A little porter came hurrying towards him, seemingly finishing his evening tea.

'I'm sorry I wasn't here to carry your bags, sir … ' The little porter looked past the biographer.

'Funny, I thought I saw a gentleman with you, sir, must be me eyesight.'

'No, no one got out with me.' He looked around at the little waiting room. It looked quiet and empty now.

'I'm afraid there ain't no car to take you into the village sir, but it's a lovely evening, and only about a mile along the lane.'

The biographer looked out from the platform across the flat salt marsh and thought of all his bags. The narrow lane crossed the railway and then meandered away between wind-bent hedges to where, in the distance the biographer could see a huddle of buildings beginning to show their evening lights at the windows.

'Not many visitors?'

'Oh no, sir, not many people comes down here, them's that likes the coast don't get much joy here. It's the pebbles you see.'

'Pebbles?'

'Yes, the beach sir, fearsome lot of pebbles, get brought up by the storms you see. People don't like sittin' on a lot o' stones do they – not conducive to a holiday fer the little 'uns, you see.'

'No, I suppose not ... '

The porter carried the bags down to the railway crossing gate in the lane.

'Not far to walk, sir – only long thereaways. Not many staying at the hotel now, season's over really – what there was of it, that is. Nice evening for a stroll though.' The brown wrinkled face smiled at him. Touching his cap he pocketed the tip and ambled back up to the platform.

The wind seemed to rise a little and picked at the biographer's coat. He held it round him and looked around at the desolate marshland. Not very inviting he thought, and picked up his luggage to walk on. A bird squawked from a bent thorn by the side of the road.

'Don't know so much about nice evening,' he muttered. It seemed to have become overcast. The lane was gullied and hard to traverse, the puddles reflected the greying sky. There was a splash behind him, one of the station-master's children he thought, and ignored the sound. Another footfall behind seemed to indicate a heavier tread, the porter perhaps – he turned, but the little station seemed far off and lonely against the dismal marshes that stretched away to the distance, it must have been a bird.

It was a little over a week later that the promised article arrived upon his editor's desk, and it was a puzzled editor that demanded to know the whereabouts of his top freelance biographer. But it seemed that no trace could be found of him after he left for Worsey the week before. The editor's curiosity was further aroused, when he read the scrawled note attached to the last page of the article. In a handwriting he did not recognise as the biographer's the unsigned note implored him to print the article, it was badly spelt and of an uneducated hand. It contained a threatening tone, he felt – not in words, but carrying a feeling of threat almost as if it were embodied in the paper itself. It was thick yellow paper of uneven texture, a type the editor had not seen before.

It was not in the editor's normal habit to take office work home, but he was concerned and uneasy about the article. Its unusual content would arouse criticism, not of the biographer but of the journal for printing it. If perhaps he could contact the biographer ... but he had tried all day, it was like trying to contact the dead themselves!

To his wife's displeasure he spent late into the evening reading and re-reading the article, he looked from article to attached note. He respected the work of the biographer, but he had his journal to think about. He finally decided he could not risk it. He put the article to one side and looked at his study clock, 11.30! His wife had already gone to bed. He would leave it – but he was certain he couldn't print that sort of thing, not even if it meant losing his most gifted contributor.

He turned out the light and walked to the door. His hand stretched towards the door-handle his fingers clutched at an unexpectedly damp, cold handle, he flinched back. The lamplight from outside the window fell full on the door, the whole door seemed to be wet with streaming water. He fell back fumbling on his desk for the light, a wind blew cold at him from somewhere. The light came on, the door was the same as always white painted, dry. The room was warm again. He told himself that he must have been overworking. He would go to bed and rest. He walked back to the door and turning the handle carefully went out into the hall. He would leave the light on, it didn't really matter. He would rest, he would feel better after a good night's sleep.

It was a drawn and tired editor the following day that instructed the article to be published. On inquiry as to his state of health his secretary was merely told to get the article published and to mind her own business.

The biographer's article caused some amount of excited speculation among friends and acquaintances, but the editor proved tight lipped and uncommunicative about both the article and the biographer's whereabouts. It was consternation of another kind entirely that the article engendered among the reading public. One of the many letters received by the journal is typical of the reaction.

> This misplaced and bizarre portrayal of the life and death of an obscure captain of the coastguards is well out of the normal realm associated with 'Insight Into'.
>
> In my own, and I believe many other readers' minds, the journal should confine itself to its normal literary work. Personally I find the article about H. Hamries as disquieting as it is unpleasant. People of the kind referred to are better left dead, buried and forgotten.
>
> I am appalled that *Monthly Review* should dig up such depravity. I would have imagined, that this month's 'Insight Into' would have been better devoted to the recent demise of a national hero and not to listing the unpleasant, and often deplorable wrongs perpetuated by an unknown who committed suicide over a hundred years ago. There is clearly no contact between an appraisal of Sir Desmond Jeffries and this foul person on whom the Journal has chosen to lavish time, money and space.
>
> Doubtless other readers will feel the same, and be more cautious in spending their own money on future publications.

The editor was still dealing with the considerable repercussions caused by what became known as the 'Harry Hamries Article' when he received a letter from the biographer's sister written on his behalf. It expressed deep gratitude for the courage and friendship the editor had shown in publishing. The letter had been written in a small nursing home in Sussex, in which the biographer was staying. The editor made his way to the address during his next weekend.

He found the biographer still ill, but recovering, from near-drowning and exhaustion. He had been badly beaten by the surge of the tide where it met the pebble ridge. He was lucky, the editor was told, to be alive. If the coastguard had not been called out he would not have been found in time. His sister had been contacted, and it was she who followed the sick man's wishes that he be transferred to a private nursing home away from the coast.

The editor was concerned to hear about his associate's health but soon turned the conversation to what had really brought him to Sussex.

'The article caused a great deal of controversy.'

The biographer moved his head wearily on his pillows –

'Yes, I suppose it did.' His face was bruised and cut, his cheeks had a grey pallor.

'How long before you will be able to get up again?'

'Oh I don't know,' – the biographer seemed uninterested – 'I'm lucky enough.'

'Lucky?'

The biographer looked up with perception in his dull eyes –

'You wouldn't have printed unless you had known, you've met him.'

He spoke of facts, he didn't give the editor a chance for denial or evasion.

'I did have some bad nightmares ... '

'Nightmares?' The biographer was slow of speech, his eyelids drooped a little.

'It doesn't matter now, anyway, you can call them nightmares. It doesn't make any difference.' He sounded tired and far away. The editor didn't answer.

'And what of Desmond Jeffries?'

The biographer looked up.

'So you knew about that?' The editor could talk about this at least.

'No, not really – you must have started from somewhere – I checked with Lady Jeffries.'

'About the file.'

'Yes.'

The biographer looked at his editor with tired eyes.

'It started there. Jeffries had promised to write it when he was a child; he even started it, but could never get it finished.'

'I suppose that's what drove him insane.' The editor was thoughtful.

'Yes, that and guilt. He was persecuted, it must have been unimaginable suffering.'

The biographer sighed. 'He's quiet now. He wanted to make his guilt known.'

'And that's what it was all about – Jeffries' death; attracting you to Worsey; even me. All for that guilt?'

The biographer looked steadily.

'Yes, isn't that enough suffering, the years of waiting?'

The editor was thoughtful.

'But he tried to drown you.'

'Oh no!' The biographer's eyes blazed. 'No, you've got it wrong, it was he who saved me.'

The controversy raged for some time in literary circles; eventually an interested historian from that part of the coast did discover that the biographer had been telling a true story. The historian's article was published two months later in *Monthly Review*. There was a coastguard called Harry Hamries. His crew of coastguards had seen the flares of a sinking ship and had set out to rescue the people on board. It is recorded that the weather was foul in the channel, and the crew of both rescue boat and the foundering craft were lost. Hamries hadn't gone out that night, the crew had tried to raise him, but he was in a drunken stupor, and was the only man left ashore; the only one to survive.

In his grief he committed suicide by drowning, there is no record of his body ever being reclaimed from the sea and there was no funeral. Apparently there was a rumour that local inhabitants had found the body and, refusing to have it properly buried, hid his remains on the marshes. But no proof of this story exists.

The historian also discovered that there had been a local story about Old Harry coming back on stormy nights, going around the village tapping on windows and doors. Apparently, as he rather disparagingly stated in his article, the belief was that Old Harry wanted to tell of his guilt. But, so the local story went, no one would let him in, or listen to his story, because he had to suffer for the wrong he had done to the village.

This information the historian had received from a very old inhabitant of the village; the hauntings, the old man said, had ceased years ago when he was a boy. It was from this old man that the historian discovered something that he did find of particular interest, the recently deceased national hero, Sir Desmond Jeffries had lived in the village about the same time the hauntings stopped, in the very house where Harry Hamries had lived. A strange coincidence considering the whole Harry Hamries debate had started because people had expected a biographical tribute to the great soldier. But of course, it was only a coincidence

X

A Trip To The Forest

Derek Stanford

It was to have been a second honeymoon: instead it became a prologue to parting, that separation we fear the most.

No man, I think, can have felt happier – more grateful to the fates and providence – when we set off for a short after-tea stroll, through the reddening gold of a September afternoon, about the village of Brockenhurst. No man, I am sure, could have felt more utterly cast-down and broken than when we returned a bare forty minutes later. My wife's complexion was still blooming, but I was glad of a late summer tan which hid, I hoped, the ashen colour of my cheeks must have worn beneath it. And, of course, my wife knew nothing of it – or next to nothing – and must not know.

We were staying in an hotel not more than five hundred yards from the woodland of the New Forest, an hotel which combined the attractions of an old country house with the comforts of central heating, a bathroom en suite and colour television in our room. We had taken an early tea, sitting on the balcony of our bedroom, the sun still warm on our hands and faces. Down below, in a walled garden, with apricot trees growing against the walls, sat one or two guests reclining in long chairs and low tables set with silver-plated tea-pots. This little enclosed part and the balconies were the best sun-traps in the hotel's wide grounds. We had only arrived that afternoon, motoring down from Town in the morning, and promised ourselves we would take our coffee out there after lunch on the morrow.

'How glad I am you brought me down here, darling,' my wife reflected contentedly. 'I'd always wanted to see the New Forest. It's where Jack Hargreaves lives, you know,' – she was an amateur naturalist and enthusiastic about his programme. 'As for the hotel, it's quite, quite perfect. Everything's perfect, my perfect old beau.'

And I had thought the same thing too, till just about half-an-hour ago. The effects of time, enhancing or deadly, may have little to do with the lengths of its duration.

*

I had planned this week's short holiday to celebrate our silver wedding. The notion of a party at our flat with friends I had put by for a little later on. My wife had only recently been discharged from hospital and I did not want her to overtax her strength. It is true that I was told by the consultant when I went to collect her that she was a new woman; and, indeed, her appearance lived up to his words. She herself protested that she was fit for a party – both preparing for it and enjoying it afterwards. On the other hand, she did not resist very strongly my plan to bear her off to the country. I said I had missed her so badly in the two months she had been away that I did not propose to begin by sharing her with sundry friends and acquaintances. This gambit of pseudo-selfishness paid off; and now she was reconciled to my plan to cosset and pet her a little. My wife knows my bent for making literary pilgrimages on the slenderest excuse, so I told her that I wanted to see Brockenhurst with its 'station in the wood' which John Davidson had written about, describing the lyrical humorous courting of a girl by a sailor on the crowded platform one glorious Easter Monday in 1907.

The sun, the earth were made for him and her,
The gorgeous weather and the holiday.

I said that, who knows, we might also strike lucky, even though we were going there in a later month and not flushed with youth like the sailor and his girl.

And it is true that, though I'm fifty-five (and my wife three years younger), I did want her on her own and did feel romantic about spiriting her off. There is nothing like absence combined with good news to exhilarate our tender feelings; and both these conditions had been granted me. Orpheus-like, I had my wife back from the underworld of the hospital. I had also been informed I was to be promoted. I work at the British Council and have only five more years' service to complete. It meant that my last stretch would be both more comfortable and remunerative. I was full of that late euphoria – that deep well-spring of content which, at times, replaces the excitements of youth. Little did I think my St Martin's summer was to be nipped so mortally with frost.

*

We had no sooner unpacked in our hotel room, with its wide well-sprung double-bed, and rung for tea to be served on the balcony, than I began casually sketching in, with splendid lordly nonchalance, the things we could now do when I retired, my pension being linked to my more generous salary. Our son Charles had taken a good degree, found himself a job and married early. We had nobody to please but ourselves, and no one who pleased us so much as each other.

I said we'd begin with two or three months in the Canaries, a place I've always wanted to visit. Then there were plans to buy a cottage in, or just outside of, Chipping Camden, that Cotswold village to which C.R. Ashbee of the Guild of Handicraft had led some fifty workers and their familes away from Town in 1902, and where a few relatives of these same men were still to be found working today. It all fitted in with my desire to live just as much as I could in the pre-Great War world.

As I talked, I patted my wife's plump knee and thought how I would pay homage to her other firm plump parts in our wide double-bed that night. Really I was extraordinarily lucky. Eurydice had vanished before Orpheus got her to the open air, but here was mine before me in a classic pale green lambs-wool twin-set, as large as life as if to mock those doctors who for some six weeks had confessed themselves puzzled by her illness.

Thinking of this, it was as if a shadow crossed the sunny lawn beneath our balcony, rolling out, as I imagined it, from that group of hornbeam trees within whose shade, I told myself, there could be the way down to Pluto's kingdom. For a moment, I remembered the manner in which, on Anne's first entering the hospital, the doctors had been cheerful but non-committal, then more and more evasive and less and less cheerful, until the time when, their backs to the wall, they had finally admitted themselves to be baffled. Then had come a period of about two weeks – an interregnum between life and death, as I had obscurely sensed it to be – in which they said as little as possible, only communicating the impression that they considered her case 'serious' and that they were busy with a new series of tests. It was only when frightened and provoked by their blank unexpressiveness, I had categorically demanded to know the truth that they confessed themselves utterly puzzled. And while they confronted this condition, I imagined Anne in her sleep descending spiral after spiral in the dark.

One night I had had a dream – or rather one same recurring dream, broken off and renewed after repeated awakenings. In my dream, I lay in our large bed at home and was on the edge of sleep when I heard the flapping of wings in the bedroom. I switched on the bedside light and was just in time to see a gigantic black moth disappear behind the curtains. I was about to get out of bed to uncover it when I actually woke up with my heart beating fast. Once more I dropped off; and, in my dream, again the black moth flapped around the room, disappearing through a sliding door of a cupboard. Once more I got up to look for it; and again found myself asleep in the marriage-bed we had shared so long together. With mounting apprehension, I closed my eyes; and for the third time sensed the huge black moth flapping in the dark above the pillow. I say 'flapping' since although this word does not generally describe the light flutter of lepidoptera, in this case it did convey the more emphatic movement of its flight. Flapping or fluttering, the insect made for the windows. Being summer, the top one was open, and through it flew this sinister creature.

In my dream, I was rising to shut the window in order to prevent the moth's return, when I woke up in my bed feeling curiously reassured.

At the hospital I was met by the first smiling doctor who had spoken to me about my wife's condition for over a month. It seemed they were 'very pleased' with her, and just as clearly pleased with themselves – though with what reason I do not know. Nor was I, somehow, surprised to learn this, my dream in its own fashion having oddly prepared me for the news. Within a fortnight, Anne was discharged. The doctors spoke, almost gaily, of the 'total disappearance of her symptoms', 'a lightning cure – yes, certainly a cure', but what quite it was supposed to be a cure from, I found it difficult to ascertain. To me it seemed rather as if she had healed of her own accord – as if some subconsious mechanism, whose workings had first made her ill, was possessed of its own time-device and had switched itself on to a new phase, a new current, at some appointed moment. Yet, here was my Eurydice beside me, far now – it seemed – from that cavernous dark passage down which she had gone and from which she had returned. Perhaps it was to remove her from that physical area where the dark god had seized her – as if he might have a lien on the place – that I had brought her down to Brockenhurst. Perhaps I believed some other deity ruled the rides and glades of the New Forest.

These fancies and fears formed a sort of passing chequer in the golden sunshine of my good fortune. An invisible branch in the brain shifted in some mental breeze, and the slight patterning of shadow disappeared. And here was Anne saying to me: 'Now we've had tea, let's take a stroll round. Maybe you'd like to examine Mr Davidson's wonderful station.'

*

So out we went to look at the village. Anne sauntered along beside me, and now with the colour back in her cheeks, I saw again in my wife, restored both to health and husband, the projection or extension of that solid plump child she had shown me in a photograph taken when she was five years old.

Brockenhurst station was disappointing. No ghosts of a sailor and his girl paraded

> the platform gallantly, their arms
> Woven in a complex lover's-and-sailor's knot

as they had that spring Bank Holiday when Davidson saw them so many years ago. Nor can I blame these shades for having removed themselves. 'The station in a wood' was in a wood no longer though there were still trees on the Lymington side. If their stage had suffered this change, why should the actors stay faithful to it?

This railway disappointment did not daunt our spirits, however. Anne always liked to explore, and the village street with those New Forest ponies wandering freely about the roadway – even leaving their droppings in the doorways of the Post Office and the Bank – intrigued her vastly. 'By special delivery' was her reference to this odd regional feature.

At one end of the village a water-splash extends across the road. The pavement is raised to span it, and Anne ran over to the other side, then, stepping down into the roadway faced about and shook her fist as if at some pursuer the other side of the shallow stream.

'Avaunt, avaunt, Asmodeus!' she cried out to someone, it seemed, just over my shoulder. I turned round, hardly expecting a demon, but wondering if any pedestrian was in line of sight to receive her challenge. Decorous as Anne habitually was, there were moments when her high spirits or histrionic urges got the better of her. And this was one of them.

'What's all this barnstorming in aid of?' I asked her.

'Don't you know evil spirits can't follow one across running water,' she replied. 'A pity I couldn't have waded through. But, then, I'd have got my stockings wet. Not that any spirits have followed us down here. I'm sure of that. You drove too fast.' She was certainly in a merry mood this afternoon.

Beyond the water-splash the village high street ended, forking right to lead back to the Lyndhurst-Lymington road off which our hotel was situated, and left in a road leading into the Forest. Some five hundred yards down this branching road stood a large late-Victorian hotel which had now become a sort of centre where the local young held their rave-ups. No more was this the haunt of parasolled picnickers cool in muslin. Did the old lounge and hall-way frown on these flitting bar and ballroom guests?

'Always living in the past,' said Anne, to whom I imparted these banal reflections.

'True,' I replied, 'but that may be better than living in the present or the future.'

'Well, we've tried the past and the present already,' retorted Anne, 'but how can you possibly write off the future without having tasted it?'

'By inference,' I answered. 'By the logic of events. And, anyway, I *feel* the future will be worse.'

At that moment, we saw the telephone box – a mere ordinary scarlet kiosk – on the pavement of the road leading to the Victorian hotel. It caught our notice because where it stood, with no fence or building behind it and the late afternoon sun streaming unimpeded across the heathland which bordered on the wood, its glass burned brightly as if on fire. Anne, who was overflowing with fancies, suddenly turned to me and asked, grinning, 'What would you do if you rang our flat and had someone answer you?'

'Tell them not to drink all the booze,' I grinned back, 'and to water our window-boxes before leaving.'

'But supposing … ' she persisted.

'All right,' I said, and stepped into the box.

*

How extraordinary to think that one's peace of mind could hang upon so harmless a jest. What would have happened if I had not entered? Would I have remained ignorant and happy, or would the information have come some other way? How can I say what would have been if the future had not gate-crashed into the present?

Of course, Anne meant it only as a game; and, attaching no importance to her challenge, wandered off the pavement to a clump of blackberry bushes growing on the gorsy heathland.

How providentially these brambles beckoned to her, I only began to realize when a voice at the other end answered my dialing with the digits of our Richmond number – 940-4240. Along with my utter amazement, an awful premonition dawned in my mind.

'Hullo,' I said. 'Who's speaking?'

'John Dowland,' came the answer – my own name – in what I took to be my own voice.

'John Dowland of the British Council?' I queried.

'That's right,' came the reply, 'and who are you?'

'John Dowland,' I told the speaker.

'I thought so,' he answered. 'We're one and the same.'

'You mean,' I said, 'you're me and I'm you?'

'Correct.'

'But,' I began, 'whatever can have happened?'

'Oh, never mind that: we can't go into it now. Listen, have you got Anne with you?'

'Why, yes, she's just a hundred yards away. I suppose she isn't with you too?'

'Well, not in the flat. She's in the hospital. Although they don't say so, I think they think she's dying.'

A terrible fear I'd possessed all the while, but which my present happiness had suppressed, surfaced in my mind and burst blackly like a large dark unfolding lily. 'What is she dying of?' I asked.

'They just don't know. They're completely baffled.'

At that moment I saw Anne turn back from the brambles whose coal-black berries she had been purloining. 'Quick, tell me,' I asked, 'what's the date at your end?'

'Twenty-first September.'

As with me. 'And the year?'

'1989.'

It was five years on. The time of my retirement.

Anne was now walking towards the box, looking puzzled in the extreme. All I had time to say was 'All right, I'll 'phone you as soon as I can;' and then she was there, tapping at the glass of the door.

'Who was it?' she asked; then 'God, you look pale. Are you all right, darling?'

I had to extemporize double quick. 'It's Mrs Huggins,' I said, naming our cleaning woman. 'Yes, I'm quite all right; but I did get a bit of a shock when someone answered the 'phone.' Mrs Huggins usually came to us on Mondays. I told Anne that she had to visit her daughter on Monday since she was due to be confined (an event I knew to be in the offing); and, having the key to our flat, decided to go over the place this Saturday afternoon instead.

Anne began to appear relieved. 'I just couldn't think who it could be,' she said. 'You looked so ghastly, too – as if you'd heard news of your own funeral.'

That was a nasty one. 'It was just that I never expected to hear anyone answer,' I told her. 'Even Mrs Huggins came as a shock.'

'Well, not to worry,' encouraged Anne. 'With all that woman's many faults, she's not something that goes bump in the night. By day, of course, it's quite another matter. Come on, let's get back. You can do me before dinner if you like. There's a band later on, you know. I feel like dancing this evening. I've never felt so full of life.'

*

Things had developed at such a speed that I'd had no time to question them. I'd stood in a 'phone-box for just two minutes and covered more ground than if I had travelled for several days by jet. What earthly dimension of space can equal those distances of the future? I thought of Pascal's fear in the face of the starry infinite night-sky and of another *pensée* of his 'Of how many kingdoms do we know nothing!'

Of the one I'd just entered I certainly knew nought. Entered so easily, so readily too. And entered with such awful consequence. Could it be re-entered was what I must discover; and that I must find out as quickly as possible. I felt it would not be so simple this time.

I had just made love to Anne, and she was making-up and dressing for dinner. She had come in from the bath after our return, opened her gold dressing-gown and posed in front of me. My normal impulse would have been to have squeezed a breast or pulled her to me. Instead, I just stood there, looking at her. Indeed, I'm not certain that I even *saw* her; and, if I did, it was not as an attractive woman expecting to be made love to, but rather as someone loved and lost, already disappearing over the horizon.

Anne had put a hand on my shoulder. 'Well, you old slow-coach? Or would you rather later?'

That brought me back from those 'infinite spaces'. Afterwards, Anne had said, 'I didn't think you wanted to, and then you almost ate me alive. It was as if you were saying good-bye to me for a long, long time. You looked so sad too. Didn't you enjoy it?'

'You know I did,' I had said, and kissed her.

Now I was down in the bar waiting for her to join me and wondering if I could possibly risk a call to our flat before she came. I decided against it. The 'phone was in the hall; and Anne would have had to cross it on her way to the bar. I should have to invent some excuse, and – what was far more difficult – account for putting the receiver down as soon as I caught sight of her. No, it would be safer later.

Safer it may have been; but easier it was not. After dinner, Anne was bent on dancing; and after dancing, drinking a little; and then after drinking, bed without undue delay. As Anne's notion of all these activities involved my presence, there was no slipping out for a short turn around or some other such alibi. That all-important call would have to wait till the morrow.

*

In the night, I thought much about what had happened. How *could* one ring a number and speak to someone five years hence? Even more extraordinary, how could one speak to oneself? I thought of Maupassant's terrifying tale *Le Horla* in which a man enters a room in his house only to find himself seated there in a chair before his own eyes. But Maupassant was suffering from syphilis whose toxins produced this hallucination.

I returned, again, to the thought that had come to me while speaking on the 'phone – namely, that the voice I heard was that of my 'secondary personality,' my *alter ego*, or even my subconscious. What, in one sense, would be more natural than that my recent fears for Anne, buried now only skin-deep, should surface and enact for me the devastating dialogue I had conducted in the 'phone-box? But, then, I had actually *rung* the number, and Anne herself had seen me speaking. Could I have been speaking merely to myself, hearing words which no one uttered – words articulated by no living lips which none the less framed my deepest fears? In other words, an hallucination? Any psychiatrist to whom I might talk would invariably come up with this solution. Yet, not for one minute could I seriously accept it. I *knew* that I had dialled our number, got the ringing tone and, finally, been answered. The mechanics of the experience precluded such an interpretation.

Was there, then, an actual pipe-line to the future, a wave-length on which it was situated? This was something I must endeavour to find out first thing in the morning. Another thought also came to me – namely that I had dwelt with my imagination so much in the past that the gods were correcting the balance and forcing me to this foretaste of the future; an action whose equity I could not gainsay.

After tea in bed, I nipped out smartly and was washed, shaved and dressed in ten minutes. Anne, who enjoyed dawdling in bed, asked me what all the rush was in aid of. Fortunately, the day had dawned fine with just that soupçon of crispness which offered an excuse for a pre-breakfast walk.

'I'd just like a sniff of air while you dress,' I told her. 'I think I'll try to get a *Sunday Telegraph*. We only ordered the other two.'

Not the 'phone in the hall, I decided; I did not want to be over-heard. I made for the box by the water-splash where such grim news had been imparted to me. I rang our number, but received no reply. After waiting five minutes, I tried again but without success. Perhaps he – or I? – was out at the hospital.

During the next five days, I rang and rang again – always without an answer. Could there, after all, be no one at the flat? Could it all have been some dreadful fancy? I would like to have believed this, but could not.

The remainder of our short holiday was very different from

what I had intended. Outwardly, we did those things which I had planned as part of our programme – a visit to Lyndhurst (depressing place), a day in Lymington (delightful town), and a short trip to the Island. The requisite spirit, however, was lacking. I sought to keep my end up, and over-acted the fantasist in my nature so that Anne should not suspect just how desolate I felt. Possibly my ploy mystified her a little since after outbursts of facetious gaiety I would sometimes swing back to a state of depressed exhaustion.

When, at length, we drove home, I was apprehensive. Mrs Huggins had somehow to be contacted and squared before Anne started talking to her. And what should I find in the flat, I wondered? Would there be any traces of the fact that it had been translated into the future? I could only hope that it had reverted to the mundane present. On that score, I need not have worried, save for one small detail.

'Look,' exclaimed Anne as we entered the hall, 'the 'phone's off the hook.' She picked it up, listened, placed down the receiver, picked it up and listened once more. 'Something the matter with the 'phone,' she reported. 'It's dead or cut off. How could that have happened?'

'Mrs Huggins,' I told her, as a shiver ran through me.

XI

The Lerryn-Brown Line

Meg Buxton

Miss Hilary Lerryn-Brown, director and former owner of the Lerryn-Brown Shipping Line, was relieved to get off the main road and take to the narrow lanes. The sun, emerging from a bank of cloud, was sliding towards the western horizon and shining straight into her eyes: it had rained earlier and the roads were still wet, the spray on the windscreen from cars in front adding to her discomfort.

Never having been to Cornwall before she could scarcely believe how narrow some of the lanes were. The one she drove along now was only wide enough for one car, with here and there a curved bay cut into the steep banks for another to pass. She found it amusing but thought it would be less so if one were in a hurry.

Hilary was not in a hurry. She had lately sold a thriving business on her doctor's orders, the shipping line of which she had been left in sole charge when her father, demented with grief at her mother's death, had made it over to her. Young as she was when she took it over she had discovered a great talent for business and had devoted her entire life to the firm, her brilliant handling of it having been responsible for its remarkable success.

It had, however, taken its toll and her doctor warned that if she didn't give it up she might well have a nervous breakdown; so here she was, the right side of forty and the rest of her life to do with as she liked.

Her ancestors had come from Cornwall and for as long as

she could remember she had wanted to visit it, to explore it and try to discover her origins but had never had time – until now. She could not have guessed how successful she would be.

The narrow lane joined a wider road at a T junction. Hilary had done enough driving for one day and decided to stop at the first reasonable place she came to for a meal and a rest; even, possibly to spend the night.

The road took her through a small, unprepossessing town, lurking dourly under the first low bastion of the moors which loomed darkly against the sunset sky. Nothing here to tempt a weary traveller to stop, but on its further outskirts a large sign caught her eye.

'Lanrose Abbey Hotel,' it said, and directed her to take the next turn a quarter of a mile down the road.

Turning the car where indicated she drove along a moorland lane until, rounding a massive outcrop of rock, she was disappointed to see a mock-Tudor edifice built of yellowish reconstituted stone, entirely out of keeping with its surroundings and complete with four-centred arched front door and diamond-leaded windows. It was just the sort of place she most disliked, but well-kept shrubs surrounded a large forecourt in which several expensive cars were parked, it looked comfortable and prosperous. She suddenly realized how tired she was: it would have to do just for one night.

The reception hall was pleasant and spacious, redolent of the chrysanthemums which stood in gleaming copper jugs on well polished furniture. A log fire burnt in the wide fireplace, a welcome sight on an evening which had turned unusually chilly for September. A fair-haired girl bent over a typewriter at a desk in the far corner and an elderly yellow labrador lay in front of the hearth, fast asleep and snoring.

The nail-headed, ornately-hinged door closed quietly behind her. Neither the girl nor the dog looked up or appeared to have her heard her come in.

'Excuse me – ' she said.

The girl glanced up then leapt to her feet, knocking papers off the desk and gazing at her in astonishment, and the old dog, lumbering with difficulty into a sitting position, threw back her grizzled head and let out a mournful howl.

The girl behind the desk recovered herself.

'I'm so sorry! I didn't hear you come in,' she apologized and, flapping a hand at the dog, 'Be quiet, Amber!'

Hilary asked about accommodation and the girl looked doubtful.

'We are very booked up at the moment,' she said, 'but there may have been a cancellation. I have only just come on duty, let me check.'

She consulted booking charts and turned back to Hilary delighted.

'Yes!' she said, 'You're in luck! Some Americans have cancelled so we have one room free.'

Hilary wrote her name and address in the register. She only used the last part of her surname, Brown: there had been quite a lot of publicity over the sale of such a well-known business as the Lerryn-Brown Shipping Line and she did not wish to be a source of interested comment on its account.

The receptionist rang for a porter to carry the cases and led the way up wide, deeply-carpeted stairs.

'This is the old part of the building, Miss Brown,' she said, throwing open a door at the end of a long passage. 'Americans always like this room.'

Hilary could well believe it. It was a lovely room; low, ornately-plastered ceiling, linen-fold panelling and four-poster bed, all genuine. She was enchanted.

'It's always known as the Abbess's Room,' the girl said as she stood aside to let the porter in with the cases. Hilary saw the man start violently as he turned to smile at her before leaving, a look of astonishment on his face.

'There's a portrait of the Abbess downstairs,' the girl went on. 'You must look at it when you come down to dinner.'

Amber's mournful howls could be heard from the hall below as the receptionist and the porter left the room and shut the door.

How odd, Hilary thought as she looked round the beautiful room; it had seemed such a brash and pseudo place at first and yet had turned out to be all she could have wished – or at least this bit had – and she liked hotels to have a dog about; she loved dogs. It suddenly struck her that this particular dog, and, in fact, these particular people, had behaved a little strangely: she was used to people being slightly taken aback by her vast bulk, but these two seemed almost frightened of her at first, and the dog had seemed positively distressed whereas animals usually took to her at once.

She was indeed extremely fat. She had lost count of the diets she had tried, the exercises she had struggled with, the health farms she had patronised in an effort to lose at least a few stone, all to no avail. Her father had been enormous and so, according to him, had been his father. She had resigned herself to her great size as being hereditary and was only very occasionally even aware of it, such as now. Shrugging her shoulders she put the odd behaviour of staff and dog out of her mind and decided to have a bath before changing for dinner.

Hilary exploited her size when buying evening clothes, choosing loose caftans and dramatic gowns with a great deal of soft, heavy material falling from the shoulders. She put on one of these now, a voluminous, shimmering grey garment, blessing modern synthetics for the way they emerged uncreased after being packed.

She clasped chunky bracelets round her wrists, hung a large pendant on a thick chain round her neck, added heavy antique earrings, which glistened beneath the coils of her abundant dark hair, and picked up a silver fox stole. She was ready to go downstairs.

The receptionist smiled at the large lady as she crossed the hall and pointed the way to the dining-room. A narrow passage, lit by wall-brackets which seemed to flicker as though they held real candles instead of electric imitations, led to the older part of the building in which her bedroom was also situated.

In the comfortable old tweeds which she wore for driving Hilary knew she looked atrocious, but in her evening clothes she was well aware that she looked magnificent. As she approached the dining-room door, from which came the smell of good food, and the hum and tinkle of conversation and gentle laughter, she drew herself up, folding her hands which held the fox fur at waist-level in an attitude of repose. She made an entrance.

The buzz of conversation stopped: the rose-silk shaded lights on the small tables seemed to gutter and dim: the discreet clatter of china from behind the swing doors to the kitchen gave way to a crashing of metal.

'Pig!' someone shouted, 'Gluttonous pig! Look at the size of her!' the men's hands clutched at her, savagely bringing her down onto the slate-paved floor.

Hilary tried to cry out but could not. Sweating, stinking men were clawing at her jewellery, wrenching it from her neck and wrists, tearing her earlobes from which hung the magnificent glistening earrings.

'Look at this ornament for a bride of Christ!' one shouted, holding up her pendant which seemed to flash lurid red, like rubies, in the light from the flaring torches held high above her by his companions.

'Bride of Christ, be damned!' cried another, taking the neck of her gown in a huge hand and tearing it from her body. 'Tonight she's mine!' and, fumbling with his clothes, his coarse, unshaven face leering with lust, he fell upon her prostrate, naked form.

Hilary fainted, consciousness returning fleetingly only for her to plunge deep into the merciful blackness again. She was fitfully aware of urgent, fluttering hands trying to pull her ruined robes about her, of stifled sobbing – 'We too, Mother, we too,' – before ribald laughter rang out again and once more, knowing that the appalling act was to be perpetrated on her helpless form yet again, and to the tune of terrified female screams all round her, she sank again into oblivion.

*

Dame Hilary's father had founded and endowed Lanrose Abbey. When her mother had died he, beside himself with grief, had given all he had, his home, his money, his daughter – and indeed his life, as he followed his wife very soon – to God.

The family mansion, itself on the site of an early Christian shrine, had formed the nucleus of the convent, and in the years during which the cloisters, the cells and the chapel were being built she had been sent to a Devonshire nunnery as a novice where the plump and terrified child had learnt what life had in store for her; a strict rule, little sleep, little food, little comfort, little love – other than the supposed love of the Almighty – and hard work.

When the new convent was complete she was transferred there, as had been her father's wish, and in due course she had become the Abbess.

Dame Hilary knew that her rule was lax, but she had never had a vocation, only a genius for organization, for controlling numbers of people and for making money. The land which was part of her father's gift was lush and productive, the farmers to whom she leased it supplied the small community with an abundance of food and their tithes went to swell the convent's already well-lined coffers.

Lanrose became a well-known resting place for travellers, the richer ones making sure of a welcome on their return by the gifts they showered on it. The Lady Abbess indulged her penchant for rich materials and costly jewelry. Her rooms were furnished almost regally and her robes, although of a suitably subdued grey, were intricately and beautifully made of the softest satins, her cloaks of furlined velvet: her plump wrists were encircled with broad bands of gem-encrusted silver and the great cross she wore held at its heart a pigeon's blood ruby. She loved animals and most of her nuns had a pet: she had a small beloved dog which went with her everywhere, nestling in her arms or sheltering in the voluminous folds of her skirts, a fuzzy grey dog whom she named Teazle, thinking that he resembled a teazle seed head.

She saw to it, however, that the offices were celebrated – and beautifully sung – at the appointed hours; saw to it that the novices, the daughters of rich local families, were fully aware of their obligations if and when they took their vows; saw to it that God should in no way suffer.

The fact that her nuns worshipped in comfort seemed sensible to her: it did not mean that they prayed any less fervently because their feet were warm, their stomachs full and their maternal instincts given rein to some extent in their love and care for their animals. The poor were lavishly fed at her gate and there was no dishonesty, no licentiousness in her establishment. God was well-served.

Managing her estates, her religieuses, her lay sisters and her domestic affairs kept the Abbess busy and content. If she ever thought of what her life might have been had her father not ordered it as he had she gave no sign, but perhaps her vast size explained in what way she compensated herself for all the normal womanly outlets she might have had: she ate and drank enormously and well at the groaning refectory table, as did the rest of her household, and had many supplementary meals sent to her private rooms.

The contented little community in a fold of the moors, well off the beaten track except for those who knew and sought it, thrived. Prayers of thanksgiving for their comfortable lot, for the love of God, and that of their Abbess, soared continuously to heaven, but in 1536 an anxious whisper of rumour found its way along the narrow lanes to alarm them.

Due to King Henry having taken the control of the English church into his own hands small religious houses were being dissolved.

Dame Hilary, the Lady Abbess, sent her spies abroad to find out more and they came back with comforting news. Only those foundations whose annual income was less than £200 were to be disbanded and Lanrose was rich, even by the standards of the larger establishments. The sixteen nuns, eleven novices and numerous lay people in her charge sighed with relief and rejoiced, but she was too intelligent to relax completely. It would be their turn next, she thought, and she started to make plans.

Some of the novices she dissuaded from taking their vows and, loading the pack horses she provided them with the most precious jewels and church ornaments that had been accumulated over the years, she sent them into the furthest corners of Cornwall, there to act as custodians of her treasures. She remained with her professed nuns, still eating well, still comfortable, but with her ear to the ground.

All went quietly for three years. The King seemed content to have defied the Pope and his own Cardinals in the matter of his divorce, his marriage to – and execution of – the infamous Anne, but then the blow fell quite unexpectedly.

Being so far from the Court, so isolated among the rolling hills, who would have expected Lanrose Abbey to have been the first to suffer under the King's second and far more disastrous assault upon religious houses?

His commissioners came one night as the nuns were about to sit down to their supper.

*

Hilary was aware of quiet voices and gentle hands.

'How did she get these lacerations round her neck?' a man asked. 'And this ear lobe has been torn right through. I shall have to stitch it.'

A voice she vaguely recognised, a girl's voice, answered him.

'She seemed to be beating off an attack,' she said. 'Of course there was no one there really but she became so frenzied that she tore her jewellery off: her necklace was flung right across the hall and we haven't even found her earrings yet. She was wearing beautiful ones, I noticed them especially.' She sighed. 'She looked quite wonderful, poor lady, all in grey and silver and carrying a fox fur – I've got that in the office, it was covered in blood but I've sponged it and it's all right now.'

Opening her eyes Hilary realized that she was in the beautiful, low-ceilinged hotel bedroom, lying in the great four-poster bed with a kindly man in glasses bending over her and gently swabbing her neck. A doctor, she thought; why do I need a doctor?

The fair-haired receptionist hovered nearby and from outside the door she heard a dog's anxious whining. Was it Teazle? She tried to sit up but firm hands restrained her.

'What happened to me?' she asked distractedly, remembering nothing, nothing but an anxiety for a little dog, a little grey dog called Teazle.

'You were suddenly taken ill on your way into dinner,' the fair-haired girl said, taking her hand.

'Lie still and don't talk, Miss Brown,' the doctor

admonished her. 'You hit your head when you fell. You have severe concussion, and somehow you have managed to collect bruises and lacerations on just about every inch of you.'

Hilary turned her aching head from side to side. Her long grey dress lay over a chair; it was torn from neck to hem, the lovely material frayed and covered in blood. How did it come to be like that? The dog outside continued to whine.

'Is that Teazle?' she whispered, clutching at the only thread of memory that might explain what had happened.

'It's Amber,' the girl said. 'I don't know what's the matter with her. I'll take her downstairs,' but Hilary implored her not to take the dog away.

'Please let her in,' she said, 'Oh, please let her in.'

The doctor nodded and the girl opened the door to admit the old yellow labrador. The dog lumbered towards the bed as fast as she could, and with a great effort raised herself up so that her front paws lay on the sheet by Hilary's hand. She stroked the grizzled head and the animal whimpered with joy.

Why had she thought of a small, fuzzy grey dog she wondered, but her mind was too weary to concentrate and the faint memory of a little animal held close in her arms faded. It was enough to have this one near, and so obviously pleased to see her.

During the week that followed the old dog refused to leave her room as Hilary gradually regained her strength. The doctor came daily: he was a local man and amused her with his store of knowledge about the countryside, history, legend and superstition. One day she asked him about the hotel. Was it ever a real abbey, she wondered?

'Oh yes, indeed it was,' the doctor replied. 'And quite a unique one. It was small but very rich, and that didn't suit Bluff King Hal at all. He dissolved it with a vengeance.' He leant back in his chair by the window. 'Of course one can't hold him entirely responsible for the brutality with which his commissioners treated the nuns. Apparently it was the worst atrocity of the whole Dissolution; even the Abbess didn't escape.'

'The Abbess?' Hilary said. 'This is called the Abbess's Room, isn't it?'

'Yes, it is,' the doctor replied. 'A magnificent room for a magnificent woman, I've always thought. It seems she had very individual views on how her convent should be run. She thought that God could be served as well, if not better, if his servants were well fed and comfortable rather than half starved and cold, and I've no doubt she was right.' He got up and walked across the room to the hearth where a small fire burnt cheerfully to offset the September chill

'She was enormously fat,' he shot an apologetic glance at his patient as she lay hugely on the bed, her face half-hidden by the dressings round her neck and about her ears. 'She obviously liked her food – and by all accounts it was excellent here, as was the wine. The commissioners' men took the greatest delight, so the story goes, in – er – taking their pleasure of her,' he shifted his foot along the slate hearth-stone to excuse any indelicacy, 'She became pregnant, poor woman, but at least she had friends further west who looked after her and the baby when it came. It was a boy, they say, who took the name of the place where he was born. How silly of me, I can't remember what it was called, I must be getting old! Some little hamlet on the south coast, I think.'

The elderly man came back to the bedside.

'Am I tiring you with my chatter?' he asked.

'No, no!' Hilary said, 'Do go on, please. I'm fascinated.'

'Well,' he said, 'it would appear that with money from the valuables his mother had had the foresight to spirit away before the disaster, and with her business acumen and contacts to help him, the young man eventually established a thriving trade with France; it seems he had quite a little fleet of ships, exporting wool and importing wine.'

'A shipping line,' Hilary said wonderingly.

'I beg your pardon?' the doctor said. 'I didn't catch what you said.'

'*And* his mother paid back every penny that the valuables were worth,' Hilary went on, unaware that he had spoken, 'to the poor, homeless monks and nuns who were wandering about begging.'

'Er – yes, I expect she did,' the bewildered man said.

'I *know* she did,' said Hilary.

The doctor looked at her in some alarm. Was her mind wandering? No, she was just letting her imagination run on a little, he thought.

Hilary's eyes stared past him to the panelled wall beyond. There was a dark, obscure painting hanging there.

'Is that the Abbess's portrait?' she whispered, pointing.

'Yes!' the doctor said, glad to get back to something more concrete. 'I'd forgotten. Mary, the receptionist, had it brought up. She thought it might interest you when you felt better.'

Hilary gazed with swollen, bruised eyes at the vast and stately woman in the portrait. The painted eyes gazed back at her from under the fur-lined hood. They could have been her own, clear, widely spaced and grey. Lapped in velvet folds a small, fuzzy dog lay cradled in the painted arms.

'Teazle!' cried Hilary and the yellow labrador on the hearth rug turned her head, tail wagging.

'I beg your pardon?' said the doctor again. 'What did you say?'

'Nothing of importance,' she said, raising herself on one elbow. 'Tell me, doctor, could the place to which the Abbess went to have her baby be *Lerryn* by any chance.'

'Yes,' he replied, surprised, 'yes, I do believe it was.'

XII

Voice From The Past

Denys Val Baker

William Hocking and Samuel Leddra were Cornish born and bred, and as befitting two Celtic patriots they had always taken a devout interest in Cornwall's history and mythology. William was a librarian and Samuel a schoolteacher, both occupations which permitted a reasonable time for reading and studying. When they were not engaged in the pursuit of ideas they often followed more active projects by attending field days and digs held by local archaeological societies. In this way they had visited the Lanyon Quoit near Madron, the ancient village of Chysauster, the Porthmeor settlement near Zennor and a number of other such monuments scattered about West Cornwall.

For some reason, however, they had never managed before to visit Castle Pednolva, reputed to be one of the very earliest settlements of its kind. Several times, in fact, they had planned such a visit, but always something had arisen to prevent the journey – one or other of them taken ill, an unexpected visit from relatives, some other call on their services.

'You know,' said Samuel one day. 'It's almost as if we're not *meant* to go to Pednolva.'

Whereupon William, who was the more determined of the two, declared forcefully:

'Tommyrot! It's high time we went then, don't you think?'

Which was how, one lovely spring day, William and Samuel at long last found themselves climbing the steep moorland path, strewn on either side by granite boulders over-grown with moss, which led to the craggy hilltop where the ancient British had built Pednolva. For some years now the Ministry of Works had been in charge of the site so that everything was pleasantly laid out, smooth lawns running between the fortifications, protective fencing guarding the deeper caverns, and unobtrusive plaques placed here and there to inform the curious holiday-makers who came in their swarms during the summer months.

But at this time of the year there were no holiday-makers, and indeed William and Samuel were the only visitors. The hut which at the height of the season contained a guide and display of appropriate literature was locked up. Over the whole site there was an air of loneliness, even of desolation. Even the slanting sunshine, silhouetting the outline of the ruined walls, seemed to strike a false note.

'Brrh!' said Samuel, shivering for no apparent reason. 'It's – it's peculiar, isn't it?'

William nodded grudgingly.

'I'll admit there's quite an atmosphere.' He pulled out the guide-book he had brought from his library shelves and began studying the plans.

'You mean, it's in a marvellous state of preservation, really. I mean, just look over there. That would have been the central courtyard. And see the way each habitation was arranged to link up. Why, you can still follow the walls. And there, part of the drainage system. Marvellous, really.'

They spent an hour wandering about the marvels of Castle Pednolva before at last climbing to the top section, with its thick granite look-out from which sentries of olden times could keep watch over the wide terrain running from Land's End to St Michael's Mount. Here William and Samuel ate the sandwiches and fruit which, as usual, they had brought with them … and afterwards, suitably replete, sat themselves down on the smooth grass, leaning against the high granite slabs which had once formed the wall.

It was hot, very hot, and where they sat the crumbling granite kept away any vagrant breezes. As they leaned back they could feel the burning sun beating upon their faces – were aware, too, of it burning into the granite all around, as it must have done down all the long, long years. They closed their eyes and gave themselves up, as they imagined, to the sunshine of this twentieth century day.

At first they dozed fitfully, half asleep, half awake. Then William – it was at first – started into wakefulness, almost as if impelled to open his heavy lids. Blinking in the brightness he had the strangest of sensations: as if nothing in that bright scene was quite the same as before. Yet when he looked more closely there seemed no pronounced change ... Only perhaps – yes, it was curious, but he could have sworn to this – only that perhaps the crumbling walls were larger, larger and higher. Yes, they really looked almost as if ... but of course, that was nonsense. He shook his head deprecatingly, and dozed off again.

It was Samuel's turn next. He had his head inclined to one side so that his eyes, when they opened, gazed out upon the long green sward. When he had first dozed off he had felt sure it had been bathed in sunshine. Now – now it was curiously darkened, as if under a shadow. For a long time Samuel stared at this darkness in growing perturbance. Then, quickly looking around, he had the same immediate sensation as William, of walls growing higher.

But of course, it couldn't be – it must be his imagination. Afraid to voice his fears to William for fear of being ridiculed, Samuel closed his eyes. But he found it impossible to doze off again.

William found it difficult, too. In fact the two of them lay there in a sort of suspended trance, neither asleep nor fully awake; both filled with growing fears and forebodings, of which they yet dared not speak. Once William opened the corner of one eye and it seemed, horrifyingly, that where there had been bright sunshine and the scent of heather, now there was only semi-darkness – and a kind of musty smell. And once Samuel half peeped and found the same enveloping shadowiness, and was too frightened to do anything but lie there with his eyes closed, trying to persuade himself it was all part of a bad dream.

But it was no dream. And when, feeling their bodies growing quite chilly, William and Samuel at last opened their heavy-lidded eyes, the sight that met their eyes was one they might well have preferred never to see. Gone was the view of crumbling ruins of ancient times. Gone was the air of genteel guardianship, the rows of fences, neat lawns, the box office. Gone in fact was every vestige of Castle Pednolva, the carefully preserved ancient monument, as they had seen it. And in its place …

'My God!' exclaimed William, seeing the white bareness of his legs.

'Heavens!' observed Samuel, discovering his own semi-nudity.

They looked at one another. William saw a slim, rather under-nourished looking Celtic warrior with a tunic made of animal skin, and sandalled bare feet. Samuel saw a similar apparition, except that William also wore a crude kind of helmet.

They stared at one another in petrified astonishment, as if at ghosts.

'It can't be – ?'

'It's not possible – ?'

But it was: it was. From outside what they now saw to be a full size building, built in huge blocks of granite, they heard sound and movement. Nervously they crept to the door and looked out upon a large circular courtyard, across which bustled other human beings … men dressed like themselves, and women, too, tall graceful women with flowing hair … One of them, carrying a pitcher of water, suddenly came over towards them, before they could hide. She showed no surprise, but smiled, handing them the pitcher, and then went on her way.

William and Samuel retreated into the shadowiness of their fortress lookout. At first they were too shocked to speak. Then, pathetically, they turned to one another, as if seeking comfort in mutual recognition.

'Samuel,' said William, hoarsely, stretching out a hand and clutching at the other's arm as if for re-assurance. 'You do – *remember?*'

Samuel nodded miserably. That was partly the trouble, indeed. They found they could remember only too well. They sat there in their tunics and sandals and they remembered ... I am really a schoolteacher, I am a librarian, we both live in Penzance and have an interest in archaeology ... and the unspoken, fearful question remained: how can we get back into our own time?

For there could be no doubt about what had happened. Twentieth-century men they might be, a schoolmaster and a librarian indeed, with pressing demands on their services – but somehow they had slipped back into time. And time now was nearly two thousand years ago, when Castle Pednolva had been a large encampment of the local Celts among whom now, obviously, they lived as members.

And were well known, indeed. That was the curious and most worrying aspect. They were obviously two of the guards who took turns in keeping a watch from the fortress lookout: they even had nicknames which were meaningless to them – but then so was the stream of words which emerged from their mouths when they spoke.

'Obviously,' whispered William. 'We have inherited the bodies and characters of two Celts of this age ... so we can speak their language.'

At the same time they remembered their English – just as they remembered many other aspects of their twentieth century knowledge. How to drive a motor car ... how to use electricity ... how to print a book ... how to operate a washing machine ...

But unfortunately most of this knowledge was useless indeed, even dangerous. Once or twice when William and Samuel forgot themselves and tried to demonstrate a simpler way of achieving some end, based on their superior knowledge, they were viewed with sudden suspicion.

'For goodness sake be careful,' hissed William. 'They'll think we are sorcerers or something.'

Gradually, over a period which might have been weeks or months – for without clocks and calendars they were lost – it became evident that such a suspicion was, indeed, being created. The men and women with whom they mixed daily in the village square could hardly be called over friendly. After a while it began to seem they were watching William and Samuel wherever they went – even following them into their dwelling place.

'I can't stand it,' whispered Samuel. 'Oh, if only we could go back!'

'Forward, you mean,' said William with a certain dry humour.

They sighed. They had done everything they could think of, sitting down in the same spot at the same time each day, closing their eyes, hoping for a miracle. But there had been no miracle, and somehow they knew there wasn't going to be one.

'Perhaps,' said William thoughtfully, 'It would help if we could write a message and bury it.'

Samuel nodded eagerly. 'Excellent, excellent.'

They looked at one another in sudden desolation.

'No pens ... no paper ... nothing.'

But twentieth century ingenuity came to their rescue. William found a sharp-edged flint and a long slate and they sat down and laboriously began compounding their message to posterity, scratching the words out as neatly and compactly as possible.

'Our names are William Hocking and Samuel Leddra, and we are prisoners in time. Please rescue us if you can ... '

When the message was written they dug a deep hole in the earth and buried it, marking the spot with a round blue slab.

*

It was the summer dig at Penwith Archaeological Society, this year being held at Castle Pednolva. A team of enthusiastic young students were led by an even more enthusiastic geology master from the local grammar school. They dug, they explored, they excavated. At last one of them gave an exultant cry, having turned back a round blue slab and picked up from underneath it a long slate, with words scratched on the surface.

Excitedly he took it over to his leader.

'Look, there's some sort of message. Fancy, after nearly two thousand years!'

The geology expert held up the slate, and sniffed.

'Use your intelligence boy. Why this is written in English! As if anyone two thousand years ago could speak English, let alone write it!'

With an expressive gesture he threw the slate away.

'Rubbish! Someone trying to play a practical joke I expect. Come along now, back to work – you never know, you might find something really important.'

And somewhere in the ghostly shades two weary Celtic warriors heaved a despairing sigh at man's inhumanity to man.

XIII

Lost Journey

A. L. Barker

The first time I saw Gerda Charles it was coming up to the fifth of November and I thought now there's a first-rate guy fawkes. She was in an orange box on wheels, parked in the high street. It so happened that the sun, slanting between Woolworth's and Sainsbury's lit up her face. When she moved, nodded and grinned, I was shocked. I have no great reverence for life, there's too much of it about, but there has to be a line drawn. It ought to be drawn this side of Gerda.

She was like those things that hang out of church gutters – hooked nose, pop eyes and a great long tongue. She was looking up into people's faces and her tongue was darting in and out as if she'd lick them up and swallow them. What bothered me was how she fitted into the orange box which was small and square. So where were her legs?

A girl came out of Sainsbury's with a loaded carrier-bag which she dumped in the box on top of the old woman. A jar of pickled onions fell out, hit the pavement and smashed. Onions rolled under the feet of passers-by. The girl and the old woman laughed. She was pretty, the girl, in a Spanish or Irish way, plump, dark-haired, white-skinned and warm. Her blouse was open at the neck, I could see her throat down to her cleavage, yet it was raw weather and most people were well wrapped up.

I had nothing particular to do, Saturday morning being my free time. I was propping up the wall outside the Grapes, when they opened I would go in and prop up the bar. The girl and the old woman and the broken pickle jar were a bit of fun, that's all they were at that juncture. I wasn't the only one looking at them and smelling vinegar.

The box was fixed into an old pram frame. I watched the girl's very nice breasts bear down on the pram handle to get the cart moving. She bumped it down the kerb, not looking where she was going. A Telecom van screeched to a standstill and the driver yelled at her. She calmly pushed the contraption across the road, the old woman put up two fingers at the Telecom man.

When they reached my side of the street the girl had trouble getting the cart up the kerb. I went to help, it bothered me to see those breasts getting bumped.

'You want to take it easy, this is a busy road.' I lifted the cart by its front axle.

'And?' said the girl.

'You nearly got your mother killed.'

'My mother!' She put her hair back from her face and looked me over. 'Fat chance,' she said calmly. 'Give us a hand up the hill, will you?'

That's how I was caught up with those two. The girl's name was Lalla, if she had another I never knew it. Gerda told me once that she herself was a cousin of Robert Dudley.

'Who's he?' I said, and she said:

'The Earl of Leicester, the Queen's lover.'

'You could be the Duchess of Dillwater,' I said, 'but I never heard of any hanky-panky in that quarter.'

'On my mother's side of the family,' she said. 'Robert and I shared a wet-nurse. And it was Elizabeth Tudor, you bloody fool.'

That came later. As I pushed Gerda up the hill that Saturday I thought here's a turn-up for the book: I wonder what sort of book it was.

They told me they lived at Charlesworth Manor. 'My ancestral home,' said Gerda, with the cackle I now know so well. Charlesworth is a mansion set in acres of ground outside the town and it's been empty for years. They were in fact squatting there.

For reasons best known to myself, and not all connected

with Lalla – Gerda herself fascinated and repelled me – I pushed the box-cart up the hill and along the lanes and the length of the overgrown, bramble-bound drive and round to a side door of the house.

'You're blown,' said Gerda. 'A young fellow like you. I'd run rings round you if I had my legs.'

'Well you haven't,' said Lalla. She took the shopping out of the cart and by accident or design the blanket came with it and I saw that all Gerda had was a pair of rusty black trousers sewn into flaps where her legs would have begun.

Those two had broken and entered the house. Boards nailed across the door frame had been prised off and used to smash the glass panels. After that it would have been easy to reach through and pull back the bolts. I could see Lalla doing it, and Gerda egging her on.

'Suppose you're spotted?' I said.

Lalla shrugged; Gerda said amiably, 'There's more than one way of killing a cat.' I wasn't surprised, the idea had already penetrated that they could take care of themselves.

Certainly they could. They were occupying a room beyond the one they had broken into, which was a sort of scullery-outhouse, and they had made a bedsitter of what must have been the kitchen, a big vaulted place with built-in dresser and a range that would have cooked a horse. They had found three broken-down armchairs and stuffed the holes with newspaper.

'Two are Lalla's, the other's mine,' Gerda said. 'I don't need to stretch in bed.' They had the original kitchen table which was so heavy that no-one could have shifted it, a tea-chest for wardrobe and packs of paper cups, plates and air-line cutlery still in polythene wrappers. Lalla opened the door of the range on a clear, hot, liquid fire. 'Plenty of coke in the cellar,' said Gerda.

They told me to come again if I liked. I didn't know if I would like until Lalla took me out into the scullery and stood close.

'How do you manage?' I said. 'Heaving her about?'

'She can creep a bit.'

I went back the next day. The weather had turned

unseasonably warm, a thick gold sun and leaves drifting down off the trees. I was on my motorbike, I knew the leaves would be falling in dead quiet and it stuck me as sinister. Then I realised it wasn't the leaves and I nearly rode past Charlesworth. I wish I had, I wish to God I'd heeded the warning.

I turned into the drive, switched off the engine and walked the rest of the way. Somehow I didn't want to advertise myself, I suppose it was a bit of a defensive measure.

They were sitting outside taking the air, like a lot of people that last fine Sunday afternoon of the year. Gerda was in the armchair which also served as her bed, the castors had cut up the moss on the brick path when Lalla dragged it out. Gerda seemed to be asleep. Lalla was on her back on the grass, hands under her head, knees cocked and swaying to and fro, sort of lazily beckoning. She was a shape to dream of, I'd had many a dream about that girl before I ever saw her.

I propped the bike against a tree and crossed the grass. She had her eyes closed, she was smiling, lips parted to show the tip of her tongue. But for the old woman, one of my dreams would have come true then and there.

Gerda wasn't asleep. She says she never sleeps and I believe her. She may shut her eyes but she's watching, I swear I've seen the glitter of her eyes through her eyelids. 'What's that?' She pointed to my bike.

'A Yamaha Tri.'

'A motorbike? Can't you do any better?'

'It's not so bad.'

'It's no good to me.' I couldn't dispute that, nor could I see why I should. 'I need four wheels,' she said.

'A try-what?' said Lalla.

Her swaying knees mesmerised me. 'It's Japanese. 981 cc's, cush drive.'

'Why haven't you got a car?' Gerda's tongue came out too. I looked away.

'I can't afford to run one.'

'You know about cars? How to make them go?'

'Sure. You switch on the ignition and release the handbrake.' It was my idea of a joke.

'Show him,' Gerda said. Lalla lay there, moving her knees. Gerda didn't raise her voice, she hurled it. 'Take him! Show him!'

'Take me,' I said to Lalla.

She raised herself slowly. When she stood upright her eyes blinked open like the eyes of a china doll.

'And me,' said Gerda, grinning.

Lalla smiled at my expression. 'Push the chair, it's easy.'

It wasn't. I was soon sweating, alternately shoving and dragging the armchair with Gerda in it, I thought any moment it would fall apart, Lalla led the way round the house, across a yard to some outbuildings which had probably been stables. When she dragged open one of a pair of double doors the roof tiles heaved like rats under a blanket.

'Inside,' said Gerda, 'get me inside.' I managed to push the chair over the threshold, nearly tipping her out in the process. I couldn't see much except the shape of something big against the back wall. 'Go on,' she said, 'it won't bite you.'

It was dark in there and smelled of winter, all the winters, no summers. Then Lalla stepped inside and either it was my fancy or she really did light up the place. I saw that the something big was a car. I went to it through drifts of dead leaves and broken tiles.

'Well,' I said, 'well, well.'

It was a Studebaker convertible, thirty to forty years old, cased like a tank, bullet-nosed, with an aeroplane mascot and chrome wing strips. It was cobwebbed all over, loaded with dust, the wheel rims squatting on puddings of rotting rubber, the hood reduced to canvas rags stuck to a rusty frame. I've seldom seen such a heap, even in the breaker's yard.

'Can you make it go?' said Gerda. I laughed, I still thought her capable of a joke. Lalla climbed on the bonnet among the bird-droppings and posed like the girls do at the motor-show. I fooled around, whipped open the driver's door. The car gave a groan and settled deeper into its rust. 'Make it go,' said Gerda.

Half a crazy old woman without a claim in the world on me, gave a totally ridiculous order and suddenly I was dead scared. 'Look,' I said, 'do you take me for a fool? Or a magician? This rubbish won't go in a million years.'

Gerda looked at me, not like a woman, even a crazy old one, more like a snake. All she said was, 'I can't wait that long,' and froze my blood.

I marched away down the drive to where I'd left my bike; if I knew what was good for me I wasn't coming here again. I sat in the saddle, my foot on the kick-start, then Lalla caught up with me. 'Do it to please me,' she said.

'You!'

'You could come whenever you fancied.'

'I wouldn't fancy.'

'No?' She pressed against me. 'Guess what it's like, alone with her, nothing to do, no telly, not even a radio. You could come in the evenings, we'd see each other as often as you like.'

'We can do that anyway.'

'In private, in there with the car.'

'What's she to you? Are you related?'

'God, no.'

'So why stay with her?'

Lalla has a way of buttoning her lip, childlike but not childish. 'That's my business.'

She was welcome to it. I wasn't drawn to her because of her beautiful nature and I didn't assume, as someone else might, that she stayed out of pity. I knew that she didn't stay as an act of charity or for any other reason. It was Gerda who kept *her*. And in my blood or my brains I sensed that I was in danger of being kept too. But Lalla drew me like a magnet. I took the risk, cocksure that I could handle it. And Lalla. I didn't begin to see that the dice was loaded.

I started going to Charlesworth in the evenings and working, pretending to, on the car. The first thing I did was clear out the back, and for a while everything went according to my plan. Lalla came to the garage and we had some very rewarding moments and knocked a lot of stuffing out of the back seat. The springs were still springy, the weather was mild, we weren't disturbed, and everything was laid on. Lalla was wonderful, the girl I'd always dreamed of having. I couldn't get enough of her. That, too, was laid on.

Then one evening she came late. I'd almost given up. Gerda,

she said, was asking questions about what I was doing.

'Tell her we've been testing the rear axle,' I said.

Lalla didn't smile. 'Think she doesn't know?'

The next evening she didn't come at all. I waited, walked around the car, kicking it. For something to do, I tried to open the bonnet. The grips were rusted solid, I battered them free. Then I fetched the storm lantern which was all the lighting there was, and looked inside.

That engine wasn't a challenge so much as a black comedy. The battery had split and leaked. Only the fact that the car was built like a steamroller had stopped the acid eating through the wheel arch. Every bit of rubber was shrivelled, the wiring was scrambled, there was a bird's nest on the sump.

I started picking out the rubbish, dead leaves, beetle-cases, straws, and the next thing I knew I'd taken a rag and was cleaning off the rust. Next thing – you've guessed – I had started tinkering. But you won't guess how soon I forgot about Lalla. I worked, really worked, stripping that engine, until nearly midnight. When I say stripping, I mean simply stripping off the muck and frass of years. The next night I took solvents and white spirit and wire wool and a bundle of rags along with me. Just in case she doesn't come, I said to myself, I'll have something to do.

She did come. We got into the back of the car and I said, 'What happened to you yesterday?' Gerda had stopped her coming, she said. I nodded. 'Tied you to the kitchen table, did she? Or just knocked you out?'

Lalla said bitterly, 'Don't be so bloody naive.'

I was annoyed and didn't give her a chance to say more. She left soon after, without another word. I hung up the storm lantern and started chipping out the remains of the battery.

I spent three evenings cleaning up the engine and I promise you I was never so hard to please. When I work on the bike I'm not fussy. I'll check the parts are back in place, the screws tight, maybe I'll wipe off excess oil and grease, and that's it. Believe it or not, I chipped, scraped, rubbed and worked on that old wreck, scrupulous as if I was cutting and polishing a diamond. I kept stopping myself to ask why. Who I was doing it for? I had the answer, I couldn't believe that either.

She came one night when I was on my back sounding the chassis with a spanner. I didn't hear her, just felt the prickle up my spine as if something crawly had got into my shirt. I looked out from under the car and there she was, in the box-cart, her beak nose aimed at me. I said, 'How did you get here?'

She showed me how she propelled herself by pulling on the wheels of the pram frame. What she lacked in strength she made up for in determination. Doubled over in her box, head down, arms flailing, she was like something trapped under a bowl. 'Where's Lalla?' I said.

'Gone into town for fish and chips. To celebrate.'

'Celebrate what?'

'The car's ready, isn't it?'

'Ready for the crusher, yes.'

She nodded, she seemed pleased. 'I can't afford to pay you, but you can come to supper.'

I said, 'I may as well tell you, this thing will never go on the road again.'

'Tomorrow you can take me for a drive.'

'Not on your life.'

'On my life,' she said, and her face shone with a sort of Day-glo light.

I said, 'I can understand you wanting to get out for a change of scene, but if it means so much to you, you could hire a car. Because even if this heap could be persuaded to move, you'd be risking your neck in it.'

She grinned, showing big yellow teeth. 'The last time I risked my neck I lost my legs. I jumped in front of a train, I was desperate. Wouldn't you be, after five hundred years?'

'What?'

'Nice legs I had. I miss them. They're dead and buried, like all my best bits. You should have seen me when I was young and whole, at Cumnor. You wouldn't have had eyes for Lalla. Or Amy.'

'Who?'

'Amy – Amy Robsart.' She was at the age when the face suddenly gapes open and you see how it's going to look when only the bones are left. 'Don't worry about my neck, no one can take that. Or my life.'

'I won't be responsible.'

'Someone has to be. You or Lalla. I don't care which. Dying's a private privilege, you might think, but not for me. I've got to take a young one with me. That's the law.'

'Law?'

'Lex talionis.'

I said, 'I don't know what you're talking about. What I'm saying is that it would cost a packet to put this ruin on the road. It's over forty years old, it's American and it's rusted into the ground. It would have to have tyres, battery, brake-linings, cylinders, piston-rods, valves – just about everything needs replacing. It would be cheaper to hire a chauffeur-driven Rolls for a month.'

'I want to ride in this car.'

'I don't.'

She propelled her box-cart forward and hit the Studebaker with her fist. 'One last ride and then comes the snapping of the traces, the end of the gay and empty journey.'

I was out of my depth and the last thing I wanted was to get into hers. 'I'll go pick Lalla up,' I said.

I met her coming along the lane with a parcel of fish and chips. As she climbed on the pillion behind me I told her, 'Gerda's mad. You ought to get away from her.'

'I'll never get away.'

'You can go any time you like.'

'No.'

'Why not?' She was holding me tight round my waist, I could smell the fish and chips and feel the warmth of it pressing into the small of my back. 'Anyway,' I said, 'she's old, she won't live for ever.'

'No?'

'Look,' I said, 'there are these couple of things everyone has to do – get born and die.'

'Do you know how old she is?'

'Eighty, ninety.'

'She's four hundred and thirty-two years old.'

I twisted round in the saddle. It was too dark to see Lalla's face. 'Great leg-pullers you two. I suppose that's how she lost hers.'

'She can't die.' Lalla's whisper tickled my ear. 'She did something hundreds of years ago, murdered someone, she won't say who, and as a punishment she's condemned to keep on living. Unless – '

'Unless she doesn't,' I said, and blipped the throttle so as not to hear any more nonsense.

Lalla shouted, 'You've heard of the Flying Dutchman!'

'That old film with Ava Gardner?'

'Film? God, you're crude.'

*

I won't say I finished work on the car, because I didn't do half what I should. I salvaged four tyres and a battery from the breaker, a friend found me some plugs. I reckoned if the thing didn't move it wouldn't want brakes, but I put in oil and petrol. The radiator pissed like a baby when I filled it. Never mind, I thought, it can't boil dry.

Every day Gerda asked was the car ready. When I told her yes, she stuck out her tongue, it might have been for glee but she looked like a lizard catching flies. 'Tomorrow we'll go for a ride,' she said.

The next day was a Sunday. I had a few drinks at the pub to set me up, then rode out to Charlesworth.

Gerda was ready and waiting in the back of the banger. Seeing her sitting there like gentry, bolt upright, her woolly hat on her head, I remembered what she'd said about being related to an earl. She scared me most when I thought she might be speaking the truth.

'Where's Lalla?' I said.

'Why do you always want to know where Lalla is? We don't need her. Drive away!'

'Not without Lalla.'

I kicked the front tyre which was bald as a coot. Gerda gave me a look which would have killed if she hadn't needed me alive. She banged on the side of the car. Lalla came out of the shadows and slipped into the front seat without a word or look in my direction.

'I can't take this on the road, it's not taxed or insured.'

'I don't care,' said Gerda.

'I do. It could put me in jail.'

'You needn't go on the road,' said Lalla, 'there's a cart-track that joins with the drive and goes for miles.'

Now I hadn't even attempted to start the engine, not out of curiosity or anything else. I had no curiosity about that wreck, it was just something I was lumbered with and struggling to get shot of. I sat behind the wheel thinking that with any luck the wheel would come away in my hands. I thought the ignition won't work, it can't, there's no circuit. 'Here goes,' I said, I sounded like my father when he used to play with me on the kitchen floor when I was small. I pulled out the choke, turned the ignition key and flattened the accelerator pedal to the floorboards.

If you know anything about motors, you're not going to believe this. There was an explosion and a sort of scream as if a rocket had been fired. That paralytic old engine started first go.

Panicking, I rammed in bottom gear and we moved with a noise like an iron foundry. Tiles, shocked off the roof, crashed all round us. We lumbered across the yard, I just managed to clear the wall of the house and we were on the drive.

If you know anything about motors you'll appreciate that the steering was diabolical. I needed to brace myself, feet on the floorboards, to hold the wheel – and I wanted my feet to operate the pedals. As soon as I dared, I changed up. The gears shrieked: something – power or fury or blue murder – belted through the chassis. The dead weight of rusty metal surged forward, we were away, breaking through undergrowth, wallowing in and out of potholes, crushing fallen branches, careering over boulders, roaring and smoking. Like a rogue elephant. And about as tractable. I stamped the brake pedal down to the floor. Nothing happened. I pulled on the handbrake. There was a noise like tearing lino and a smell like a tar-boiler. The car shied slightly and kept on going.

I spend a lot of time now trying not to think about certain things: I try not to think about that ride. It took twenty years off my life, burned them off in minutes. I'll never be young again.

My only consolation, though I had no chance to savour it,

was the fact the we weren't on the public highway. If other people's lives weren't at risk, ours were. I clung to that wheel, bracing my legs till they were ready to break, fighting to engage a lower gear and slow us down. I was sweating the slimy sweat of fear, my body slipped about under my clothes, as potent as a wet paper bag.

'Can't you go any faster?' Gerda was beating the back of my seat, in another minute I thought she'd beat me, ride me like a jockey. Her face in the mirror had that grinning glare.

'Can't you drive?' said Lalla. She too was smiling.

They had perfect confidence in me or they simply didn't care. Either way I was on my own.

The driveway had become a rutted track running through beechwoods. The trees, stripped for winter, had put iron-hard roots across the track. Every time we hit them at speed I expected we'd overturn, and burst into flames. I already saw the fire, heard my own screams. Suddenly I knew why Gerda reminded me of guy fawkes. She was programmed to burn, and me with her.

The track, which had been level, started to descend. The car picked up speed under its own weight. It seemed to exult. We swooped into blackness. I thought we were running through a railway tunnel. The headlamps, of course, didn't work. I prayed, 'Holy Mary, Mother of God – ' I'm not Catholic, it just seemed more hopeful to appeal to a woman.

'It's like the Tunnel of Love!' cried Lalla.

'Faster, faster!' shouted Gerda.

Then we were out into space, and light which was more than daylight. Even in the state I was in I knew it for the cold flat light off the sea. The awful din, the grinding and groaning of the chassis, the clattering of the doors and mudguards and bonnet flaps, subsided a little, we were running across downland turf. But the engine was working itself to a frenzy. I prayed to Christ – a man might be better able to understand our situation – that it would blow up. I knew where we were – on Pendarrow Head. It's a narrow spur of cliff and we were belting across it to the sea.

I pumped at the brakes. The pedal snapped under my foot. I tried to get into lower gear and got into neutral. Sick with horror, I felt that bloody car leap forward like a greyhound out of the trap. Straight for a one-hundred foot drop to the rocks.

I didn't see Lalla get out. The next I knew, the offside door was batting to and fro on its hinges and the passenger seat was empty. I wrenched the steering-wheel from side to side to try to slow us. I wasn't reasoning straight, but I hoped if we turned turtle we just might stop rolling before we got to the edge.

That car wasn't going to slow and it certainly wasn't going to stop. If I wanted to live, I knew I had to get out. Fast. I let go of the wheel, ready to throw myself over the side. But I couldn't. I couldn't move. Gerda had me by the shoulders, she gripped me from behind with a strength I would never have credited her with. She was shouting in my ear, 'Faster, faster!' Maybe it was, 'Bastard, bastard!'

We came off Pendarrow Head at sixty miles an hour, me wondering how I'd die, feet up, or head down. It couldn't be too quick, it couldn't be quick enough.

As a matter of fact, I'm still waiting. We hit the water in a belly-flop, I remember seeing walls of water standing up all round me. Then came blackness, and roaring in my head, and the cold that kills. Death is everywhere at once – I found that out. Something was taking me down, and it wasn't only the weight of the car. I know now that it was Gerda. She had her hands on my shoulders, forcing me to go with her to the bottom of the sea.

True, the dice were loaded against me, but I have a life expectancy and I didn't mean to lose it to Gerda. I went berserk down there on the sea-bed, I bet they've never seen anything like it before. I literally smashed my way out of the car, I broke off the steering-wheel and kicked in the dash.

But I couldn't get away from Gerda. Her fingers dug into my bones. I carry the marks of her nails to this day. It was the car that saved me. The bottom fell out, I was sucked down, torn out of Gerda's grip by the weight of the engine.

They say you surface three times before you die of drowning. The hell you do. I came up just the once, and if I'd gone down once again it would have finished me. When I got the air in my lungs I drank it, swallowed it, scoffed it wholesale. Then I struck out with arms, legs, everything I had.

What I had was mostly panic. I was scared of drowning and scared rigid of drowning with Gerda. I knew that she was somewhere underneath and it wasn't the sea clawing me back, it was her.

The tide was in. It rolled me to and fro like a lump of bladderwrack, for anyone watching it must have been a laugh a minute. Somehow I got a footing on a knife-edge of rock. Next minute it sheared into my chest as I was flung down. But I held to it for dear life, and when the waves screeched back over the shingle I got my knees where my hands were. While the next waves swamped over me, I clung on, when they receded I crawled over the rocks to the beach.

There wasn't time to rest. The sea was licking at the base of the cliff. In the high days of summer, picnic parties, kids with buckets and spades, Lilos and rubber dinghies, frequent this beach. A path has been cut into the cliff for their convenience. And mercifully for me.

I scrambled up it. I wouldn't want a dog to feel like I did then, soaked to the bone, sea – or tears – leaking from every pore. My breathing deafened me. I dragged myself up over the cliff and fell on my face.

I could have died there, I wouldn't have minded dying on my own. The bitter wind sweeping across the headland, and something else – a feeling that I was watched, got me to my elbows. I propped myself on my arms and looked around.

Lalla was reclining on the grass a few feet away. 'You might have killed her,' she said.

I managed to croak, 'What about me?'

'It was what she hoped.' Lalla was eyeing me with distaste. 'God, you're a mess.'

I said, 'I nearly drowned, I'm half dead, and she's all dead – '

'Fat chance.'

'What?'

Lalla pointed out to sea.

I'll be able to see what I saw then till the day I die, whether my eyes are open or shut. I see it now. The old car was floating – yes, floating right way up – just beyond the rocks. In the back sat Gerda. She took off her woolly hat and waved it.

'Mother of God! – ' who else could I say it to? – 'She's not drowned!'

'Of course not,' said Lalla. 'You didn't stay with her.'

'Stay with her!'

'You were meant to. She was all set to die, but she can't unless she takes someone with her.' It wasn't distaste Lalla was eyeing me with, it was dislike. 'Someone young, lover-boy.'